THE LOST BOOK TRILOGY

the book of
Good &
Evil

KATHY LEE

© Kathy Lee 2009
First published 2009
ISBN 978 1 84427 368 3

Scripture Union
207-209 Queensway, Bletchley, Milton Keynes, MK2 2EB, England.
Email: info@scriptureunion.org.uk
Website: www.scriptureunion.org.uk

Scripture Union Australia
Locked Bag 2, Central Coast Business Centre, NSW 2252, Australia
Website: www.scriptureunion.org.au

Scripture Union USA
PO Box 987, Valley Forge, PA 19482
Website: www.scriptureunion.org

All rights reserved. No part of this publication may be reproduced, stored in a retrieval system, or transmitted in any form or by any means, electronic, mechanical, photocopying, recording or otherwise, without the prior permission of Scripture Union.

The right of Kathy Lee to be identified as author of this work has been asserted by her in accordance with the Copyright, Designs and Patents Act 1988.

British Library Cataloguing-in-Publication Data.
A catalogue record of this book is available from the British Library.

Printed and bound in India by Thomson Press India Ltd

Cover design: GoBallistic
Internal design and page layout: Author and Publisher Services

Scripture Union is an international Christian charity working with churches in more than 130 countries, providing resources to bring the good news about Jesus Christ to children, young people and families and to encourage them to develop spiritually through the Bible and prayer.

As well as our network of volunteers, staff and associates who run holidays, church-based events and school Christian groups, we produce a wide range of publications and support those who use our resources through training programmes.

1 The castle

I woke suddenly, with no idea where I was. A trumpet was sounding. I could hear shouts and the sound of hurrying feet.

"Jamie, wake up!"

A hand pulled back a curtain and light came into the darkness around my bed. I sat up slowly. The bed was huge, curtained all around with red and gold cloth. And suddenly I remembered... I was in the king's castle at Embra.

"Jamie! The king has sent for us. Get up!" It was my friend Rob.

"What's going on?"

"The servant said there's a Norse ship in the harbour. There are soldiers going down there right now, to bring the Norsemen up here. We're to be in the Great Hall before they come back."

Rob ran to the window and struggled to open the heavy wooden shutters. I went to join him, rubbing the sleep from my eyes.

From our high tower we could see the city spread out before us - islands and sea, towers and walls, hundreds of smoking chimneys. Embra was enormous! I still couldn't quite believe I was actually here. It was a long way from my home on a quiet island in the far north-west.

I looked where Rob was pointing, towards a harbour in the shelter of a hill. There were several ships of the king's fleet lying at anchor. And I could just make out a dark, low-lying shape, with a white flag – the flag of peace – fluttering at the tip of its broken mast.

A Norse ship! What was it doing here?

The Norse raiders were our enemies and they were growing in strength. Rob and I, along with a girl called Ali, had discovered their hidden base on the Straits of Ness. This was why we'd come here – to warn King Andrew. We were afraid the Norsemen might be planning to attack Embra.

"I bet they've come to spy on the city," said Rob. "Taking shelter from the storm – that's just an excuse."

"Why were they allowed into the harbour?" I asked.

"They could have crept in last night, at the height of the storm."

I heard the trumpet again. In the open space in front of the castle, lines of blue-coated soldiers were forming up. Then, to the beat of a drum, they began to march down the street that led towards the harbour.

Someone knocked on our door. It was a servant bringing us some breakfast. This made us forget about the Norsemen, for we were both starving. There was hot porridge, like at home, but also some strange, pale-coloured bread, and enough cold meat and fish to feed my entire family. Between us we ate the lot.

"We ought to get going," said Rob. He was restless; he liked to be on the move.

Rob was 13, just a few months older than me. He had red hair, as red as a fox, and more freckles than a trout's belly. We'd been friends for years, but Rob had always been the one who decided what we did. Maybe it came from being a chief's son.

"We don't know where to go, though," I said. "Where is the Great Hall?"

"We can ask somebody," he replied.

But we didn't need to. A servant was waiting outside our door. He led us down a twisting stair, across a courtyard and into a vast room, where our voices seemed like whispers in the emptiness. And still we went on, through a door that was hidden in the panelling and up some more winding stairs.

"If that wasn't the Great Hall, is there another even bigger one?" I muttered to Rob. "I can't believe this place."

The servant opened another door, and showed us into an odd-looking room, with walls only on three sides. On the fourth side, you could lean on a wooden railing and look down into the huge hall below.

"King Andrew will be with you very soon," the servant said, and left us there.

A moment later the door opened and we got ready to bow to the king. But it was only Ali who came in. She was looking very smart, in a brand new uniform of the king's fleet. (Although she wasn't much older than us, she had served as a cabin hand on the king's ship, the *Castle*.)

"I made the servants get me a new uniform," she said, looking pleased with herself. "I couldn't keep on wearing that ragged, dirty old thing. It was a disgrace to the fleet. Why didn't you get them to find you some new clothes?"

I told her, "We had other things to think about. There's a Norse ship in the harbour. That's a bit more important than new clothes, wouldn't you say?"

Ali ignored me, as she often did. "How's your shoulder, Rob?" she asked.

"Not too bad." But, as he moved his right arm, he winced with pain. He had a two-day-old arrow wound in his shoulder. I knew he was worried that it wouldn't heal properly, leaving him unable to fight with sword or spear.

"You should go to a doctor. We have good doctors here in Embra, and the best ones work for the king. You ought to ask to see one. Why don't you? If you don't want to ask, I will."

That was the trouble with Ali – she was so bossy. She often annoyed me. I had been half-hoping that we wouldn't have to see her again, now that we had reached her home here in Embra.

"I wonder why we've been brought here," said Rob.

As he said it, King Andrew came in, followed by Sir Kenneth, his chief adviser.

When we met the king the previous night, he'd been dressed in ordinary clothes, and I thought he looked a bit like Rob's eldest brother. Now, wearing a crown and a magnificent purple cloak, he seemed like a different person, stern and proud.

I made a nervous bow. It wasn't the sort of thing I'd been brought up to do. My people were poor farmers and fishermen, but on our island we never had to bow to anybody.

The King grinned at us. "I thought I'd better dress up to impress the Norsemen. They'll be here soon and I'd like you to take a good look at them. See if they look like the ones you saw at the Straits of Ness. See if you think they belong to the same nation."

"What do you mean – the same nation?" asked Rob.

"The Norsemen have different nations and different languages," Sir Kenneth said. "Not all of them are raiders and thieves. Some are peaceful traders. But, after the last war, all Norsemen were banned from Embra and these are the first to come here in ten years."

Rob and I looked at one another doubtfully. How on earth were we supposed to tell one Norseman from

7

another? It had been dark when we saw the first lot. We had been hiding in the forest, scared out of our skins.

King Andrew said, "But stay out of sight. We don't want our visitors to think they're being overheard. And now I'd better go and be ready for them."

2 Raiders or traders?

Sir Kenneth – a thin, grey-haired, serious-looking man – stayed with us. The king went down into the hall. Soon he was seated on a huge, carved chair, raised above floor level on stone steps. A line of soldiers formed a guard on either side. And there were several other people – translators, Sir Kenneth said, who could speak the Norse languages, and scribes who could write down what was said.

There was the sound of trumpets and drums. A line of soldiers came marching into the room, followed by about a dozen Norsemen.

There were a couple of women too. One was young and very beautiful. In the gloomy hall, her pale golden hair was like the gleam of sunlight through dark clouds.

Even surrounded by well-armed soldiers, the Norsemen didn't look afraid. They looked like strong men who would stand their ground against ten times their own number.

King Andrew greeted the strangers, and a woman translated his words into their strange-sounding language. But it was soon clear that her help wasn't needed, for the Norse leader could speak our language.

"Why did you come here?" King Andrew asked him. "You must know that my father, King James, banned all Norse ships from Embra ten years ago."

"Sir, we did not choose this. We sailed for Durham, far to the south of here, but the storm took us. Our mast broke in two pieces. We thought we were going to die. Then we saw the lights of your harbour."

"Weren't you afraid that you would be turned away, or even attacked? You should know that my people have no love for your people."

"But it was not my people who made war with Embra. It was the Sea Serpents from the fiords and mountains. That is a harsh land. After the seas rose up, there was no farming land left, only mountains. And so the Sea Serpents go out raiding."

The king made an impatient movement of his hand.

The Norseman said, "My lord, I am not a friend of the Sea Serpents. They raid my people too. We come from East Gotland. We trade in iron and copper."

As they went on talking, I was looking carefully at the Norsemen. They were tall men, with fair hair and beards. Most of them wore jackets of leather. To me, they looked exactly the same as the ones who had invaded the Straits of Ness, except that they carried no weapons.

"The Norsemen we saw had axes and swords," I whispered to Sir Kenneth. "These ones are unarmed."

"Our soldiers made them leave their weapons on the ship," he said.

Ali said, "There were no women on the ship that we saw. Why are the women here?"

"Shhh," said Rob. "Listen."

The Norse leader said that his name was Harald Haraldson and the young woman was Valda, his daughter. He was taking her to Durham to be married to an English lord. This news made people frown – the English were old enemies of Lothian.

"Look," Ali whispered. "The king likes that Valda woman – I can tell. He can't take his eyes off her."

Sir Kenneth beckoned us towards the doorway. We went out onto the stairs, where we could talk more easily.

"Well?" he said. "Are they the same, these Norsemen?"

"It's hard to know," said Rob.

"I can't see any difference," said Ali. "But if they came here to spy, why would their leader have brought his daughter? He must have known it would be dangerous."

I had a sudden thought. "Maybe if we could look at their ship, we could tell you more."

"Excellent idea," Sir Kenneth said.

Sir Kenneth sent us off with two soldiers to escort us to the ship. I wondered why he thought we needed them. We knew where the ship was. We just had to walk down the long hill towards the harbour.

But the main street, which had been empty during last night's storm, was crowded now. There were stalls and shops down each side, selling everything I could think of, plus a lot of things I couldn't even name.

"Best French lace! Best French lace!"

"Spices from the east! You can't buy cheaper!"

"Mackerel! Lovely mackerel, straight off the boat!"

The fish didn't smell as if they came straight off the boat. In fact, the air was full of bad smells. But nobody else seemed to notice. Maybe it was something you got used to after a while.

I kept wanting to stop and look around. Tall houses towering above us with narrow alleys between them... women filling water-jugs from metal pipes... a blind boy begging for money... a rich man with servants carrying him along on a chair...

"Come *on*, you two," Ali said crossly. It was all right for her – she had been born in Embra. None of this was new to her.

The crowds got thicker as we went down the hill.

"Half the city wants to see this Norse ship," one of the soldiers grumbled, shoving people aside with his spear-shaft.

At last we reached the quayside. There were several soldiers guarding the Norse ship, stopping the crowds from getting too close. But they let us through when our guards gave them the orders from Sir Kenneth.

The ship lay still in the calm waters of the harbour. But anybody could see that it had been through a storm. The mast, made from a thick tree trunk, had been snapped like a twig. Rags of torn rope trailed over the ship's side. Somehow, using only the oars, the Norsemen had managed to bring their ship safely to harbour.

"This isn't much like the ships we saw in the Straits of Ness," said Rob.

"That's because it's not a fighting ship. It's built to carry cargo," said Ali. "Broad in the beam, see? And only four sets of oars. It wouldn't be nearly as fast as the longships we saw."

I had already noticed that. And something else – this ship didn't have a monster's head at the front. It had a high, curved prow, but no fierce, sharp-toothed, grinning dragon face to send fear into the heart of an enemy. It definitely was not a warship.

"Do you think the Norsemen are telling the truth, then?" I asked Rob.

"I'd say they are. We'd better get back and report to Sir Kenneth."

The soldiers led us back up the hill. Rob was still looking around, interested in everything.

"This is an island, isn't it? This part with the castle and all the houses. Is that a separate island over there?"

"Yes. There are seven main islands," the soldier told him. "And a dozen smaller ones."

"What was Embra like before the seas rose up?"

"Hundreds of years ago, they say, it was all one city. No islands, just hills, with buildings in between. A bit before my time, that was." He grinned.

I found it hard to take this in. To me, the city looked enormous, but it must once have been far, far bigger. That was in the time of the Ancestors.

There are all kinds of tales about the Ancestors – our great-great-great-great-great grandparents. People say they had amazing knowledge. They could heal every kind of sickness, they built machines that were as clever as people, they could even fly in the air (so people say).

But there was a price to pay for all this. In the time of the Ancestors, the world began to heat up. In the far north, ice started melting, and the ocean level began to rise. For years and years, the seas went on rising, flooding the best farmland and drowning the great cities that the Ancestors had built.

Because there wasn't enough land to grow food for everyone, many people died. Others were killed, fighting over the land that remained. When at last the sea level stopped rising, life had changed. There were far fewer people alive on earth. And much of the Ancestors' knowledge had been forgotten.

Here in Embra, though, there were reminders of the Ancestors wherever you looked. It was the Ancestors who had built the castle, the tall houses, and the stony road beneath our feet. In Embra, there were still books from the time of the Ancestors, and people weren't afraid to make use of their knowledge.

My granny always said it was unlucky to talk about the Ancestors. They had come to a bad end. Talk about them, or even think about them too much, and the same might happen to you.

She would have hated Embra. She wouldn't have wanted to set foot on any of its seven islands. Bad luck would come of it, she would have been quite certain.

But we were here now. Would Embra be lucky for us, or unlucky?

3 Testing

We were taken straight to see Sir Kenneth. When we told him our thoughts about the Norsemen, he looked relieved.

"We should still watch them carefully, though," Rob said. "They might be spies as well as traders."

"Oh, they'll be carefully watched all right," Sir Kenneth said. "They will stay here as the king's guests while their ship is being repaired."

"Right here in the castle? Isn't that a bit risky?" I said. "They could find out a lot just by being here."

Sir Kenneth said, "We can keep a close eye on them here. Their ship is well guarded, and we'll make sure it isn't repaired too quickly."

"Not until the king's ships are well on their way to the Straits of Ness?" asked Rob.

He nodded. Then he said, "I'd like the three of you to be there when the ships' captains meet to plan the voyage. You're young, but you seem to have wise heads on your shoulders."

So, later that day, we were called to a room where the captains had gathered together. The king himself was there, along with Sir Kenneth and several other advisers. We kept quiet and sat in a corner. Among such important people, even Ali was a bit overawed.

"That's the admiral of the fleet," she whispered. "I've only ever seen him once before."

Soon we were called on to describe the place where we'd seen the Norse settlement. Rob pointed it out on a map, as well as he could, for the map was an ancient one from the time of the Ancestors. The coastline had changed a lot since the map was made.

Rob said, "The problem is, the Norsemen's base is on a long, narrow inlet of the sea. You can get to it from the north-west or the south-east. And whichever you choose, the Norsemen would see you coming and escape in the opposite direction."

"Then we ought to attack from both sides at once," the admiral said. "We could split the fleet – half to go westwards by Forth and Clyde, and the other half to sail up the east coast. They would trap the Norsemen between them."

A captain said, "But how would they make sure they attacked at the same time? If one group got held up by bad weather, it would be disastrous."

"Our scientists may have something that would help there," said King Andrew.

One of the men went to a table by the window, where there was a piece of strange machinery. It was the size of a lobster pot, but made of metal, with knobs sticking out here and there. I could just imagine what Granny would say: "That looks like something from the time of the Ancestors. Don't touch it! It's unlucky."

"This is called a radio," the man said. "We've constructed it using a book from the Old Times. It's only at the testing stage. Would you like to hear it in action?"

The captains exchanged glances. They looked uneasy.

But the king was full of enthusiasm for the machine. He explained that it had to be connected to a wire – a thin piece of metal – leading up to the highest point of the castle. Someone else had another machine a mile away, in the tower on Calton Isle.

The scientist spoke into one of the machines. A moment later a voice, crackly and odd-sounding, came out of the other one. "Calton, hearing you loud and clear. Over."

Now the king leaned over the machine and talked to it. He said, "Please fly a red flag, just to prove our message got through to you. Over."

"Understood," came the crackling voice.

People moved towards the windows, which looked eastwards across the city. Ali pointed out a tower built on a hill. For a few moments, nothing happened, but then a small red square appeared at the top of the tower. The flag was flying.

"That's amazing," the admiral said. "How many of these machines do you have? And how far can they send their messages?"

The scientist said, "We only have three radio sets at the moment. As for the maximum distance – well, we don't really know yet. The furthest we've tried is about 20 miles. And the message was as clear as the one you just heard."

"Three machines," the admiral said. "One for the eastern fleet, one for the western and one here in Embra so that we can let you know what happens, Your Majesty."

He was looking excited, although some of the captains still seemed doubtful. "Witchcraft," I heard one of them mutter to himself.

The talk now turned to the task of fitting out the ships for their journey. My mind began to wander. If only I could go on the voyage, to see the king's ships in action!

Suddenly, the king said, "I wish I was going with you." He had a look of longing on his face.

"Your Majesty, you can't possibly leave the city at a time like this," Sir Kenneth said, alarmed. "Imagine what would happen if you were killed in the fighting. You don't have a son or daughter to take the throne. There would be chaos and civil war."

"I suppose you're right." The king sighed. Then his glance fell on the three of us. It was as if he guessed what we were thinking.

"Admiral Crawford," he said, "will you need any of these youngsters to sail with you? They are the only people who have seen the Norse settlement and lived to tell the tale. They could help you to find the place."

The admiral stared at each of us in turn. Facing his sharp gaze, I tried to look strong and brave and reliable. I got ready to say, "15," if he asked my age. Would he believe me?

I needn't have worried; he never asked our ages. He told Rob and me to report for duty at the docks the following day. Ali was assigned to his own ship, the *Dolphin*. This pleased her so much that she couldn't stop smiling, even as she was saluting her new commander.

After the meeting, Ali wanted to go and see her family, who didn't even know she was back in Embra. She said, "They've got a shop down the Lawnmarket. You can come and meet them, if you like."

"All right," said Rob, and I tagged along too. I was curious to see Ali's family. Were they all as bossy and argumentative as she was?

We walked down a long flight of steps to the lower level of the castle. At the bottom, I suddenly realised that Rob wasn't with us. He was still halfway up the steps, leaning against the wall.

I ran back up to him. His face was paler than usual and there was sweat on his forehead.

"I don't think I'll come with you," he said. "I don't feel too great."

"What's wrong?"

"My shoulder. My shoulder hurts."

"You need to get it looked at by a doctor," Ali said. "I *told* you."

"No!" he said fiercely.

"Why ever not?" asked Ali. "Can't you afford it? I'll get my dad to lend you the money."

"It's not the money. It's because they'll stop me going on the voyage."

Ali and I looked at each other.

"That's just stupid," she said to him. "You could get really ill, if the wound gets infected. You could *die*. It nearly happened to me, remember? Don't risk it. See a doctor."

"She's right," I said.

"I never thought I'd hear Jamie say that," Ali said, grinning.

A spasm of pain twisted Rob's face. He rubbed his shoulder with his good hand.

"All right," he said. "You win."

And so it came about that, when we sailed away from Embra, Rob was left behind.

4 Wind and weather

The *North Star* was sailing through rough weather. I leaned on the rail, feeling a bit uneasy in my stomach. Surely I wasn't going to be seasick! I was used to the sea. I'd sailed in fishing boats since I was about 5 years old.

But this was no fishing boat. This was a warship of the king's fleet, carrying 12 cannon and a troop of soldiers. It was commanded by Captain Stuart, second in line to the admiral. Three other ships were sailing astern of us.

We were travelling up the eastern coast of Scotland. The admiral, with four ships under his command, was taking the shorter route, up the west coast. I wondered how Ali was getting on. Would she be able to recognise the entrance to the Straits of Ness? "All these hills and islands look the same to me," she used to complain.

It was easier for me, although I had never visited this eastern coast in my life. There were far fewer islands and inlets of the sea. But that meant fewer sheltered places when the weather turned stormy. Like now.

I told myself I mustn't be sick. If I was, I would never hear the last of it. The other boys on the ship – cabin boys and deck hands – already looked down on me. I was untrained, with no uniform and no official job to do. They thought I was just a useless passenger who got in their way.

I wished Rob was with me. I felt lonely without him.

The last time I saw him, he was in a place called a hospital, which was full of sick people. The doctors had cut open his shoulder and taken out a piece of arrowhead and then stitched him back together. "Like an old sock," he said and laughed, stopping suddenly because laughing was too painful.

"Get better soon," I said. "I'll see if I can send you a message on that radio thing." I knew he would be desperate to hear what happened to us after we sailed away.

To this end, I had got to know the man who operated the radio on board ship. Graham was his name. He was much friendlier than the sailors. Although he was still a young man, he walked with a limp because his left leg was weak. To strengthen it, he wore a brace made of metal and leather.

"What's wrong with your leg?" I asked him. "Were you born like that?"

"No. When I was about two, I got an illness called polio. Have you heard of it?"

I shook my head. On the remote island where I grew up, we had lots of other diseases, but not that one.

"I thought the doctors in Embra could cure all kinds of illnesses," I said.

He laughed. "Even the Ancestors couldn't cure polio. They knew how to stop people catching it, but as far as we know, they couldn't cure people who got it. Anyway, I was lucky – I didn't die, and I can still walk. And my father was able to pay for me to go to school, so I learned to read. Now I don't have to sit begging for money at the roadside. I work for the king." He said it with pride.

Graham spent most of his time in the small cabin that held the radio machine. I was able to help him by turning the handle that powered the machine, while he moved the little knobs and spoke into the mouthpiece, and waited for a reply. So far, everything was working perfectly, although we were now many miles from Embra and even further from the other fleet.

"How did the scientists learn to do this?" I asked.

"It was all in a book from the Old Times. The king has quite a collection of books – you know what books are?"

I nodded. "I used to have one myself."

That took him by surprise, for books were rare and valuable things. I told him the story of finding the book in an abandoned house, far away to the north-west.

"You can read, then?" he said.

"No, but my friend Rob can. He read me some of it... about a man called Jesus who lived long ago. You wouldn't be interested. There wasn't any mention of machines and things."

"What happened to the book? Tell me you didn't throw it away!"

"Of course we didn't throw it away. We gave it to the king."

"Good." He smiled. "Every book that we discover can be vital. So much has been forgotten! For a long time, people thought it was unlucky even to talk about the Ancestors. But here and there, books have survived. And knowledge survived with them."

I said, "Don't you think it might be dangerous to dig out all the Ancestors' secrets? I mean, some of them really might bring bad luck."

Graham thought for a moment. "Knowledge itself isn't good or bad. It's like a sharp knife. You can't call a knife good or bad – it all depends how you use it."

"The Ancestors didn't use it well," I said. "They made the seas rise."

"But we won't make the same mistakes as they did," he said.

The radio crackled into life. "*Dolphin* calling *North Star*. *North Star*, are you receiving me? Over."

"Receiving you loud and clear, *Dolphin*. Over."

They exchanged information about weather and position and speed. The admiral's fleet had seen no sign of any Norse ships. On our coast, we had seen a couple of trading vessels, but no longships.

"His Lordship's starting to think we're chasing wild geese," said the voice from the machine. "What do you think? Over."

I was furious. Didn't the admiral believe us?

"It's not a wild goose chase," I said loudly to the machine. "I saw the Norsemen with my own eyes. And pretty soon you'll see them too."

"Unless they've slipped past us among all these islands," the voice said. "They could be at the gates of Embra by now. Control will radio us to say the city's in flames." He paused for a moment. "But at least we've proved that the radio works! Over and out."

The storm passed over to the south of us, and the wind gradually died away. This would slow us down badly. You couldn't use oars on a ship the size of the *North Star*. Unlike the Norse ships, it relied completely on the winds.

From radio messages, we knew that the other fleet had reached the south-western end of the Straits of Ness. The ships were on patrol, ready to attack any Norse ships that came near. But they wouldn't sail into the Straits until we had reached the north-eastern entrance. At this rate, that could take days.

By the third day of calm, the sailors were getting restless. I heard a couple of them talking about the radio.

"It's unlucky having that machine on board."

"Yeah. See that wire running all the way up the mast? I don't like it. It's spoiling the wind."

"Talking to people a hundred miles away, too... it's not right. Not natural. We should put that radio man ashore and leave him there."

"The luck would change then, all right. We'd get the winds we need."

I wanted to laugh. Ali had called my people stupid for believing in good and bad fortune. But these Embra sailors were just as bad. They thought different things were unlucky – that was all.

Did they mean what they said, though? Would they really put Graham ashore and leave him there? I told him everything I'd heard and he had a word with the captain.

Captain Stuart called all the crew together. In a long speech from the upper deck, he reminded them of what people had said a few years ago, when the first cannon was brought on board ship.

"The sailors hated it. They said the whole ship could explode when a gun fired – remember? They said the weight of the guns would be enough to sink us. And they started muttering about the Ancestors being unlucky."

A murmur went through the crowd, but the captain ignored it.

"Nobody now says the guns are unlucky. We've all got used to having them on board. We've seen what amazing weapons they are. And, in another few years, you'll get used to having a radio on board. One day, every ship in the fleet will have one – so I don't want to hear any more talk about how unlucky they are. Do you hear me?"

I don't know whether the crew would have been convinced by this. But, before the captain had finished speaking, the wind began to freshen and the slack sails billowed out.

We were moving again. And soon I would see those guns in action.

5 No answer

$\mathcal{A}$ day later, we had reached the Straits of Ness. I was pretty sure this was the right place, although I'd only seen it from the opposite end. It was a long, narrow inlet of the sea – so long that it disappeared over the far horizon, and so straight that it might have been made by one slash of a giant sword. There were steep hills on both sides.

Somewhere along the Straits lay the Norsemen's base. But the wind was against us. Our ships would have to sail back and forth, tacking into the wind, changing direction each time they neared the shore.

Meanwhile, the other fleet would have the wind behind them, speeding their journey. But if they arrived at the Norsemen's base without us, they might be outnumbered. That could mean disaster. Even the ships' guns might not swing the battle in their favour.

Our captain talked to the admiral over the radio. It was decided that the admiral's fleet would hold back for a few hours to give us time to get going.

We made slow progress down the long, straight inlet. In a few places, we saw farms which must have been raided by the Norsemen. Not much was left of them – just burnt-out buildings and empty fields.

I was on the lookout for the places I had seen a few weeks before – the ruined castle on one shore, and the sheltered bay on the other side where the Norse settlement lay. But there was no sign of them yet. On and on we went, as the long summer evening faded into dusk.

At last, the captain gave orders that we should moor for the night. It wasn't safe to sail unknown waters in the darkness.

We awoke in the morning to find that the wind had changed. It was in our favour now; it would be against the other fleet. Captain Stuart wanted to talk to the admiral, to discuss plans.

I helped Graham to power up the radio. But something was wrong.

"*North Star* calling *Dolphin*; are you receiving me? Over."

No answering voice, just the hiss and crackle of the machine.

"*North Star* calling *Dolphin*. I repeat, *North Star* calling *Dolphin*; are you receiving me? Over."

Still nothing. We stared at each other in shock. Was it simply a problem with the radio – or could something terrible have happened? Could the admiral's ship have been captured or sunk?

"I'll try calling Control in Embra," said Graham. But there was no answer from Embra, either.

"Maybe the radio can't work when there are mountains in between," the captain suggested.

"Or maybe the problem is closer to home," Graham said grimly. "Jamie, I want you to check on the aerial wire that goes up the mast. Make sure it's still in one piece."

"I'll send one of my men up," Captain Stuart said.

"No, let Jamie do it."

I knew why he said that. He didn't trust the sailors – he thought someone might even have cut the wire on purpose.

I started climbing the rigging. I'd seen the crew do it often enough; they made it look easy. But it wasn't easy at all. The rope ladder sagged under my weight and, even at anchor, the ship was restless. And the mast was so high! If I fell to the deck, I could kill myself!

The best thing was not to look down. I climbed higher, concentrating on checking the wire. All right so far... The higher I went, the harder the wind blew. I held on tightly to the ropes.

At last, I reached the small platform near the top of the mast. There was a boy on watch up here, trying not to grin at my slow progress. But he wasn't unfriendly.

"It took me longer than that the first time I was sent up the mast," he said.

Still holding on tight, I began to look around... and I forgot to be afraid. You could see for miles from up here.

And what was that, far along the shore – that grey shape, half-hidden among trees?

"The castle," I breathed. I still couldn't see the Norse settlement. But I knew it had been fairly close to the castle, on the opposite shore.

I managed to get down the mast a lot quicker than I'd gone up it. "We're only three or four miles from the Norse base," I told the captain.

He looked worried. Now, more than ever, we needed the radio. Graham had taken the back off the machine and was fiddling around with the workings inside. But whatever he was doing, didn't help.

"The aerial wire seems all right," I said. "What's gone wrong?"

"I don't *know*," he said impatiently. "I had a list of different checks to make if we have problems. But I can't find the list. I'll just have to try and remember."

Captain Stuart said, "If you can't fix the radio, we have no way of knowing when the admiral's fleet will arrive. It's vital that you put it right. Keep trying."

"Captain!" It was one of the cabin boys. "The lookout reports smoke rising to the south-west. He thinks it could be a signal, sir."

We went to see. A thin line of smoke was going up from a wooded hill, a mile or so away from us. Not long after, another thread of smoke started rising further along the valley.

"Definitely a signal," the Captain said. "The Norsemen know we're here. Well, there's no point delaying any longer. We'll just have to hope the admiral makes good speed."

The captains of the other ships, the *Dragon*, the *Cannongate* and the *Golden Eagle*, were summoned to a meeting with Captain Stuart. I was called in to describe what the Norse settlement had looked like. I did my best, although it was now several weeks since I'd seen the place.

"We have to expect that the longships will come out to attack us," Captain Stuart said. "They don't have guns, so they'll have to get close enough to use arrows, or more likely try and board us."

The captains made their plans. Since we still had no contact with the admiral, Captain Stuart was in command. The *North Star* would lead the other ships into action.

As the ships lifted anchor and got under way, there was a rush of activity. A team of gunners prepared each cannon for firing. The soldiers loaded their rifles - smaller guns that fired pieces of metal called bullets.

I had seen these rifles being used in target practice, when the soldiers shot at a floating barrel. Their bullets could travel much further than arrows, but reloading was slow. I could have fired three arrows in the time it took to reload a rifle.

I longed for a weapon of some kind. If there was to be fighting, I didn't want to just stand there, unarmed and helpless. I wanted to be part of it.

Going below decks, I found the ship's armoury and asked if there was a bow that I could use.

"I think we've still got a couple of bows put away somewhere," the armourer said. "Not much call for them nowadays."

He went away, and came back with a bow and some arrows. It was bigger than my old bow, but I could bend it all right. I took it up on deck and fired a few practice shots at a dead tree on the shoreline. My third arrow hit it smack in the middle – probably just luck, but it made me feel good.

Now I was ready to fight. So why did my stomach feel all churned up? Why was my heart racing like a runaway horse?

"Cheer up, son! We're going to hammer them!" said one of the soldiers.

"When the gunfire starts, the Norsemen won't even know what hit them!" said another.

They all thought it was going to be easy. But they were wrong. A terrible shock lay in wait for us.

6 Gunfire

The lookout boy was still at the top of the mast, and at any moment I was expecting to hear that the Norse ships were in sight. But we sailed on further and further, with no sign of our enemies.

Where were they? Apart from those signal fires, there was no proof that the Norsemen were there at all. The wooded shores slid past endlessly. The ruined castle was easily visible now, and I could see a headland on the opposite shore. Beyond it, might lie the bay where the Norse ships had been beached.

Graham carried on struggling with the works of the radio machine. "It would be so much easier if I had that test plan," he muttered. "I've looked everywhere. But I can't find it."

Without the radio, we couldn't even guess where the other fleet was. We couldn't get instructions from the admiral. Captain Stuart would just have to do the best he could with what he already knew.

The other ships were in line astern, with gun ports open, and soldiers on deck ready to attack. We got closer and closer to the pine forests of the headland. Once we rounded it, we ought to be able to see the Norse settlement.

Suddenly, a loud booming noise thundered across the water. High on the headland, a puff of white smoke drifted out from the trees.

"That was cannon fire!" cried one of the soldiers.

"From the land? But the Norsemen don't have guns!" I said.

The gun, or another one, boomed out again, and I heard a dreadful cracking sound. A cannonball had struck our mast. Slowly, like the fall of a great tree, the upper half of the mast toppled over in a tangle of sails and rigging. The lookout boy went with it, screaming in terror.

The ship, which had been so well organised, was suddenly in chaos. The helmsman couldn't see what lay ahead. Men ran here and there, trying to cut free the damaged ropes and sails. Our guns fired, but too low – they were set to aim at other ships, not at hilltops.

Another cannonball crashed into the stern of the ship. It struck above the waterline, or it could have sunk us.

The wind was taking us closer to the tip of the headland. The captain shouted orders, and the helmsman tried to obey. But the damaged ship was beyond his control. With a frightening lurch, the *North Star* ran aground in shallow water.

At least the guns couldn't hit us here, close in under the hill. We would just have to wait until the tide rose high enough to float the ship again. Until that happened, we were trapped.

And now, from around the other side of the headland, the Norse ships appeared, dark and menacing. They moved swiftly, propelled by long rows of oars. Although they were far smaller than our ship, there were so many of them that they could surround us, like a pack of wild dogs around a wounded stag.

Our cannon roared. Two of the longships were hit, but the others were still coming on. We couldn't possibly fight off all these Norsemen! They would board us. In hand-to-hand fighting, we would be totally outnumbered.

Our other ships couldn't sail in to help us because they would come under fire from the guns on shore. Captain Stuart looked up at the hilltop, and his face was grim.

"We have to silence those guns, or we're done for," he said.

The lieutenant in charge of the soldiers had made the same decision. "I'll take some men ashore," he said.

"Go quickly, before we're surrounded," the captain said.

Lieutenant Reid shouted his orders. About 20 men scrambled down rope ladders into the water, which was only waist deep on the landward side. They carried their guns at shoulder height to keep the gunpowder dry.

Suddenly, without even realising I had made a choice, I found I was following them. Better to take action than just stand there waiting to be attacked!

The hull of the ship hid us from the approaching Norsemen. Reaching the shore, we ran into the shelter of the forest. The lieutenant looked around, counting his men. Then he saw an extra one – me.

"Do you know what you're doing with that bow?" he asked me.

"Yes, sir." That wasn't quite true. The bow was new to me and I would need a lot more practice to get used to it.

"All right. But don't shoot until I give the order. Ready, everybody?"

We went up through the forest at a crouching run. Towards the top of the hill, Lieutenant Reid held his arm out to stop us. The trees were thinner here. Further along the hillside, I could see two guns, with a group of Norsemen around them. Much nearer to us was a single warrior, standing guard.

"We'll take them by surprise, if we can," the lieutenant whispered. "But we need to get rid of that sentry first. Come here, boy. Think you can take him out with an arrow? It will be quieter than a gunshot."

I put an arrow on the string and took aim. The Norseman didn't even look towards us; he was gazing down at the battle scene below. He didn't seem very old, maybe not much older than me. He wore a leather jacket that was too big for him, and carried a spear.

My mouth was dry. This wasn't like hunting deer or wild dogs. I couldn't just wound the Norseman – I had to kill him straight away or his cries would alert the others.

"Get on with it, lad," muttered Lieutenant Reid.

I let fly... and missed completely. The lieutenant sighed. But I grabbed another arrow, corrected my aim and fired again.

This time I had better luck – the arrow took him in the throat. He staggered and fell with hardly a sound.

"Beautiful," said one of the soldiers. "Well done, son."

I felt weird – proud of myself and also rather sick in my stomach. I had never killed a man before.

As we crawled forwards on our stomachs, I had to pass quite close to the Norseman. He lay sprawled in the undergrowth, his eyes staring blankly up at the sky. One moment he was full of life... the next, he was dead and gone. Because of me...

But there was no time to think about that. We crawled closer to the enemy, until we were within firing range for the soldiers' rifles. The Norsemen never saw us. They were too busy reloading the cannon.

When the soldiers were ready, the lieutenant gave the order. The rifle shots rang out all at once, and several enemies fell down. The remaining Norsemen – half a dozen of them – let out a yell of rage, snatched up their weapons and came running towards us.

The soldiers couldn't reload in time to use their rifles. They drew their swords against the Norsemen's battle-axes. The two sides met with a clash of metal. I had no sword and my arrows were useless now. I didn't want to shoot our own men by accident. So I crouched in the undergrowth, keeping out of the way.

There was no doubt that the Norsemen were brave. Although we outnumbered them, they fought on fiercely until the last man went down.

Finally, there was silence on the hill. Lieutenant Reid, bleeding from a cut across his brow, counted his men. Four were dead, and almost all the others wounded.

But we had captured the guns. They were out of action now, and our other ships could come to the aid of the *North Star*. It wouldn't be a moment too soon. The Norsemen had managed to board the ship, and I could see fierce fighting on deck.

"Go up to the top of the ridge and see what's on the far side," the lieutenant ordered me. "Then come back and report to me. But be careful – there may be more Norsemen about."

As I went, I heard him tell his men, "Right. We're not taking any prisoners. Make sure none of these Norse swine are left alive."

I felt glad he hadn't ordered me to take part in this – slaughtering wounded men like animals. I went up the hill and didn't look back.

7 Gunpowder

At the top of the hill, I looked down through the trees to the other side of the headland. I knew what I expected to see – the Norse settlement.

It was there all right, with wooden huts half-hidden among the trees above a sheltered beach. Two longships still lay on the beach, with men all around, preparing to launch them. And in the middle of the bay, a ship was anchored – not a Norse longship, but a sailing ship. To me, it looked like one of the king's ships. It was battered and war-torn; there was no one on deck.

Was this where the Norsemen had got their cannon... from a captured ship?

Then I looked to my left, and saw another cannon in a clearing among the trees. A few Norsemen were standing there idle. At the moment, there was nothing for them to fire at. But when – or if – the admiral's ships came in from the south-west, that gun would be well-placed to attack them.

I ran back to Lieutenant Reid and told him what I'd seen.

"Slow down, boy. I can't hear you when you gabble like that."

"They've got another cannon! Over on the far side of the ridge!"

He took in the importance of this at once. "How many men are there?"

"About eight."

We had an equal number of men still on their feet – the rest of our men were wounded from the fighting. Could we possibly capture the other cannon? There was no one to help us. All the other soldiers were on board ship, fighting for their lives.

"Load your rifles," the lieutenant ordered his men. "And you, boy, get yourself a sword. Davie there won't be needing his any more."

I picked up the dead man's sword. It was sticky with blood. The lieutenant must have seen the look on my face.

"Don't worry, son. You'll get used to the killing. The more you do it, the easier it gets – you'll see."

"Yes, if you live that long," muttered one of the soldiers.

We went along the top of the ridge, keeping undercover, until we were above the Norsemen. Lieutenant Reid made his men spread out so that they could fire from different directions. He told me to be ready with my bow.

I could see the Norsemen not far below me. They were talking in their own language, and laughing about something. I took careful aim, choosing a tall man who stood with his back to me. But my hand, usually so steady, was shaking.

He's your enemy, I told myself. *He would kill you without thinking twice. Come on! Pull yourself together!*

The soldiers were all in position, ready to shoot. The lieutenant raised his arm. Then he brought it down again, and the guns roared. My arrow leaped from my bow. It hit my target on the leg.

Success! I shot again and then once more, before I had to snatch up the sword to defend myself. Two warriors had come charging up the hill towards me. One flung his spear – I dived sideways, feeling a searing pain in my arm.

Terrified, I scrambled to my feet again. I was no good with a sword. I hadn't a chance against two Norsemen. They would kill me!

Just before they reached me, a shot rang out, and one of the men toppled backwards. The other raised his battle-axe, his face full of fury.

The first blow of his axe knocked the sword out of my hands. The second would have crushed my skull. But, before the axe fell, the lieutenant was right behind me. "Stand back!" he shouted.

He had a small gun in his hand. He fired at close range, and the Norseman fell, howling in agony.

"Come on then, lads! To the cannon!" the lieutenant shouted.

We ran down to the clearing. The soldiers kicked aside the bodies of dead and dying Norsemen. We had done it – we'd captured the cannon.

"We could turn the gun against them, sir," one of the soldiers suggested. "If we roll it across to the rocks there, we could fire at their base."

"Good idea, soldier. But I don't think we're going to have time for that." Lieutenant Reid pointed down towards the bay.

The Norsemen on the shore must have seen or heard our fight. Now, shouting their battle cry, the whole gang of them was massing to attack us – maybe fifty men. There was no way we could hold *them* off.

The lieutenant tapped my shoulder. "One last job you can do for me," he said quite calmly. "Get rid of the gunpowder. Then the cannon will be useless to them."

"What should I do with it?"

"I don't care! Hide it – dump it in the water – just get rid of it! Now!"

I picked up the small wooden barrel, feeling a stab of pain in my injured arm. On board ship, I'd seen how carefully the gunners handled this gunpowder stuff. But I had no time to waste on being careful.

I darted into the trees. Frantically, I looked around for a hiding place. That big patch of bracken – that would do. I pushed the barrel deep in among the tall stems and leaves.

But then I remembered the other guns on the far side of the ridge. I should get rid of the gunpowder from there, too. Or should I go back and fight along with Lieutenant Reid? That would be the brave thing to do, the sort of thing that songs were written about, when all the heroes were dead.

I ran up to the top of the hill. Looking down, I could see the lieutenant and his men loading their guns. They were a pitifully small number against the crowd of Norsemen coming up the hill towards them.

Maybe I could do both things: hide the gunpowder first – then go back and fight.

The two cannon on the other side of the ridge were as we had left them. One of our men, badly wounded, lay beside them. He called out to me, but I didn't stop. I knew I couldn't help him.

There were two barrels of powder. I grabbed the first one and hurried down the hill, hiding it where the woods were thickest. All the time, I could hear cannon fire from out on the water. Just for a moment, I stopped to look through the trees.

Most of the Norse ships had now abandoned the *North Star*. They were trying to get close to our other three ships, close enough to board them. With the *Dragon*, they had succeeded – I could see fierce fighting on deck. The *Cannongate* and the *Golden Eagle* were having better fortune. Their guns were still firing, keeping the longships at bay.

You couldn't say that either side was winning the battle. But, if the Norsemen recaptured their cannon, everything could change in an instant.

I ran back to get the other barrel of gunpowder. As I snatched it up, I saw something out of the corner of my eye – a movement on the skyline. A spear hissed through the air.

I don't know how many Norsemen there were – I didn't stop to look. I ran, and the Norsemen came after me, yelling. Still clutching the barrel, I dodged between the trees.

Hide the powder, Lieutenant Reid had said... but I had no time, they were close behind me. Or dump it in the water...

I raced downhill. Somehow, I made it down to the shore without tripping up. Then, with the last of my strength, I heaved the barrel into the water. It didn't sink, but bobbed up and down, as if mocking me. Would the gunpowder still be usable if the barrel got wet?

I was past caring. I had no more strength to run, and I was trapped between the Norsemen and the sea.

There was only one place to go – into the water.

8 The turning tide

I ran along a line of rocks until the water looked deep enough for a dive. Another spear fell just behind me and I wasted no more time. Taking a deep breath, I dived and swam underwater as far as I could.

When I had to come up for air, I saw that the Norsemen had stopped chasing me. They'd seen the barrel of gunpowder. One of them waded in and grabbed it. Then, in triumph, they carried it back up the hill.

They would start firing the guns again. If they hit the *Cannongate* and the *Golden Eagle*, it would all be over for us.

I stayed afloat for a while, treading water. I didn't know what else to do. My weapons were gone. I was all alone and scared, and I felt as if my strength was leaking out of the wound in my arm.

What was I supposed to do now?

I couldn't stay in the water for much longer. I would have to go ashore. But where? There were Norsemen on shore. And by now, I was pretty sure that the lieutenant and his men must have been defeated. Probably, they were dead.

I swam closer to the *North Star*, which was still aground in the shallows. There were no longships here now. All the Norsemen had gone to join the battle out on the water. That must mean there was no one left alive on board our ship.

A couple of dead men drifted past me. One was a soldier. The other was a Norseman, floating face upwards, with a gunshot wound instead of an eye.

That was enough for me. I had to get out of the water. I swam closer to the shore, looking for a place where I could hide in the trees. And then what would I do?

"Jamie! Over here!"

The voice, hardly loud enough to be heard, was coming from the *North Star*. And now I could see a pale face looking out of a porthole. It was Graham.

I swam closer, glad to see someone I knew who was still alive. The ship was tilted over at an angle, and the porthole wasn't too high above the waterline. I might be able to help Graham get out and swim ashore, even with his bad leg.

But I soon found that Graham didn't want to get out. He wanted me to get in.

"You have to help me, Jamie! I've found the test plan for the radio. I might be able to get it working again, but I need you to take a new aerial wire up the foremast."

"Are you crazy? The ship's been overrun by Norsemen, and all you can think about is the radio?"

He said, "I need to make contact with the admiral's fleet. If I can warn them about the Norsemen's guns, then they won't sail straight into danger, like we did."

Maybe he wasn't crazy after all. And maybe the *North Star* was the safest place to be at this very moment. Graham lowered a rope, and I managed to get up to the porthole and climb inside.

The radio cabin was in chaos, with everything tilted to one side. "That's how I found the instructions," Graham said. "The paper must have slipped down between that chest and the wall. When the chest slid sideways, I saw it at once."

"How did you escape from the Norsemen?" I asked him.

"I locked the cabin door and kept quiet. It was no use me trying to fight. I thought it was more important to stay alive and get that message to the admiral."

He started rummaging around and came up with a coil of wire.

"Here, take this. Let it out as you go. Climb up the foremast, as high as you can. Probably, there's not enough wire to get right to the top."

"What if there are still some Norsemen on board?"

"I don't think there are any, not now. I'd have heard them."

Cautiously, he unlocked the door, and I looked out. In the narrow passageway, there was nothing to see, and no strange noises apart from distant cannon fire. All the same, I didn't want to go out there. I found I was shivering, partly with cold from my soaking wet clothes, partly from fear.

"Go on, Jamie! I can't test the radio without an aerial!"

I went to the far end of the passage and looked out. A dozen dead men lay on the bloodstained deck beside the wreckage of the main mast. Apart from them, the ship seemed empty.

The foremast, like the whole ship, was leaning at an angle. It wasn't as tall as the main mast had been, but I felt dizzy just looking up at it. Maybe I had lost too much blood from my arm... Maybe I would get halfway up and then fall...

I took a deep breath and started to climb the rigging. It wasn't easy, carrying the coil of wire – I nearly dropped it more than once. And I was tired – so tired. I just wanted to lie down quietly and rest.

Higher and higher I climbed, until I could see out over the water. The battle was continuing. All around the *Cannongate* was a swarm of black longships, like flies around a piece of meat. The Norsemen were boarding the ship. That left only the *Golden Eagle* still holding off the enemy, but for how much longer?

The wire was running out. I tied the end of it to a loose-hanging rope. Then, very slowly, I got myself back down to the deck. The dizzy feeling ought to have stopped by now, but it hadn't. I stumbled back to the radio cabin.

Even before I reached it, I knew Graham must have succeeded in fixing the machine. I could hear that crackling voice from the *Dolphin*.

"... we knew about the Norse guns. We were trying to warn you, but we couldn't get through. We've put most of our soldiers ashore to attack the settlement from the land. When they've got control of the guns, the fleet will come in. What does the situation look like at your end?"

"It's not looking good," said Graham. "The Norsemen have taken two of our ships."

"Make that three," I said. "Or pretty near. They're boarding the *Cannongate* right now."

"Any sign of our land attack?" asked the voice from the *Dolphin*.

"I don't think so. I'll go and have a look," I said.

From the deck, I looked up at the ridge. Something had altered in that direction. The sky! Everywhere else, the sky was blue, but beyond the headland, it was smoky grey. Great clouds of smoke were going up from the direction of the settlement.

And now I could hear the sound of rifle fire. Among the trees, I caught glimpses of blue – men in blue uniform, advancing over the ridge.

I hurried back to the radio.

"Our soldiers are up on the ridge! They must have captured the Norse base and set fire to it!" I gasped.

"Excellent. We'll be with you very soon," said the voice from the radio.

"Get here quickly," said Graham, "or it won't be soon enough."

He stayed by the radio. I went outside to see what was happening.

The Norsemen appeared to have noticed the smoke from over the hill. Several longships broke away from the sea battle and started heading back towards the base.

Then the cannon up on the ridge started firing – but this time they were firing at the Norsemen. Two of the longships were sunk before they rounded the headland.

And now I could hear cannon fire from a different direction. The sound drew nearer. The Norse ships came back into view, fleeing as fast as their oarsmen could row. Four great warships followed them, with guns booming.

The tide of the battle had turned. The Norsemen on the *Cannongate* leaped back on board their ships and headed away up the Straits of Ness. The *Golden Eagle* became hunter instead of prey, joining the admiral's ships in pursuing the enemy. I watched them from the foredeck until they were out of sight.

9 The aftermath

The following day, the admiral's fleet returned. They had managed to sink several more Norse ships, but at least six had got away unharmed.

"It would have been different if the wind had been in our favour," Ali said. "We were having to tack all the time. The Norsemen got so far ahead that they were out of cannon range. We still followed them, but then they reached the sea and went off in different directions."

"If only the original plan had worked," I said, "we could have trapped them all between the two fleets. But everything went wrong."

A clean-up operation was going on aboard the *North Star*. Ali was part of the gang that had been sent over from the admiral's ship and I was glad to see her, even when I ended up helping her to scrub the decks.

A few of the *North Star's* crewmen had survived by jumping overboard when the Norsemen overran the ship. They came out of the woods in ones and twos. They seemed almost ashamed to be alive when Captain Stuart, Lieutenant Reid and so many others were dead.

Now they were working to make the ship seaworthy again. When the tide floated it off the mud, they towed it away from the shallows and anchored it safely. They cut down the main mast from the *Dragon* to make a temporary mast for the *North Star*. The *Dragon*, less fortunate than the *North Star*, had run onto rocks and had a huge hole in one side.

The admiral had decided that there was no point trying to save the *Dragon*.

"Get all the weaponry out of her; that's the main thing," he had ordered. "We can't have any more guns falling into the hands of the enemy."

Ali, coming from the admiral's ship, had heard all the latest news. She told me how the Norsemen had got hold of the guns. As I thought, they had captured one of the king's ships – it was actually the *Castle*, which Ali had once sailed on. Not a warship but a survey ship, it had been sent out to explore the north-western coast and make new maps. It carried four cannon, just in case of trouble.

But when the *Castle* explored the Straits of Ness, there was more trouble than four cannon could handle. A dozen longships had appeared out of nowhere, captured the ship and killed half the crew.

The Norsemen had seen that the guns could be powerful weapons. What they didn't know was how to fire them. But among the captured crew was the master gunner, along with his young son, who was learning the trade.

Ali said, "The Norsemen threatened to kill the crew one by one, unless they explained the workings of the cannon. The youngest would be first to die. So, trying to save his son's life, the master gunner showed the Norsemen how to fire the guns. He didn't think it would matter. The *Castle* didn't have huge supplies of ammunition on board. He thought the Norsemen would use it all up pretty quickly, just messing about."

"Messing about? The Norsemen don't mess about," I said. "What an idiot! Thanks to him, we lost two ships and dozens of men. We nearly lost the whole battle."

"Yes, and he didn't save his son. The Norsemen tied the boy to a raft and used him for target practice. They made the father watch while they did it. Then they killed him too."

"How do you know all this?" I asked.

"Two of the prisoners managed to escape. They went south-westwards, hiding in the forests along the edge of the Straits, hoping to get back to Embra eventually. And then they saw our fleet and hailed us. They told the admiral everything."

Captain Stuart could have had that information too, if only the radio hadn't broken down... if only Graham had been able to find the instructions... if only, if only...

"You know what's really worrying?" said Ali. "The *Castle* had four guns on board. And so far we've only found three."

"So?"

"So maybe the Norsemen shipped the fourth one out earlier. They might sell it to the French or the English, or pay them to make copies of it. Those guns were great weapons when we were the only people who had them. But, if our enemies get hold of them..."

"Guns are no use without gunpowder," I said. "Do you think the master gunner told the Norsemen how to make powder?"

"He couldn't have. Only the king's scientists know how to make it," said Ali.

"Well then, no need to worry," I said.

A week later, we set sail for Embra. We had done what we could to make sure the Norsemen never returned to the Straits of Ness. Their base was completely destroyed. The forest all around it had been set on fire, to drive out any warriors who were hiding there. The soldiers shot them as they fled from the flames.

Countless numbers of Norsemen had been killed in the fighting or drowned when their ships were sunk. But on our side, we'd lost over 200 soldiers and crew. Many more were wounded, some so badly that they didn't seem likely to survive the journey. (My own injury was just a flesh wound, the doctor told me as he cleaned it with a burning liquid that felt more painful than the spear.)

We left behind us the wreck of the *Dragon*, nine sunken longships, and a scarred, burnt hillside. And many graves.

The voyage back was not easy. Sailors from other ships helped to crew the *North Star* and the *Castle*. This meant that all the ships were short of hands. Fortunately, the weather was calm, or we might have lost more ships and men.

We could be said to have won a victory, but somehow no one was celebrating.

"We won, but we didn't finish them off," I heard a sailor say. "That means they'll be back."

"Aye. The Norsemen always come back," his friend answered. "You can never get rid of them. Like cockroaches." And he spat into the sea.

I leaned on the stern rail, looking back. Away to the north-west, beyond islands and hills, lay my home, Insh More. I'd promised to be back there before harvest. But it was harvest-time already, and I was a long way from home. Soon it would be winter, the time of storms, when it wouldn't be safe to go to sea... even if I had a boat.

I wished I had some way of getting word to my family that I was still alive. And what about them – were they all right? Would they manage to get the harvest in without my help? Had they caught enough fish to last them through the winter?

Suddenly, I was longing to be back there. My island, with its quiet hills and empty beaches, was such a peaceful place... no guns, no slaughter.

"You'll get used to the killing," Lieutenant Reid had told me. But now he was dead.

And I couldn't get used to it. I couldn't forget that I had killed a man. *He was your enemy*, I kept telling myself, *it doesn't matter*.

But he still came into my dreams at night. I could still see his bloodstained body and his dead eyes staring blindly at the sky.

10 Going back

The first thing I saw, as we sailed into Embra harbour, was the Norse trading ship. It had a new main mast, which was just a bare tree trunk with no sails attached to it. How could the repairs be taking so long?

I soon forgot about it, for I had worries of my own. I didn't know where to go next, or how to find Rob. Graham had tried to send him a message for me, but word came back from the Embra radio controller that he wasn't at the hospital any more. I had no idea where he'd gone.

Graham was looking worried too. He was expecting to get into serious trouble with his boss.

"But it wasn't your fault the radio broke down," I said.

"I should have been able to fix it. It was only a loose connection to the commutator. If only I hadn't lost the instructions! They'll probably fire me. And I'll never get another job like that one." He looked down at his bad leg. "I'll end up begging on the streets of Embra."

"Me too, most likely," I said. "I've got nowhere to live and no money."

"You'd be no use as a beggar. You're too healthy-looking," Graham said, and he laughed bitterly. "It would be better if you'd lost an arm or a leg in the fighting."

Maybe I should go back to the castle. But I didn't think I would have the nerve to do that on my own. What would I say to the guards at the gate? "Hi, I'm Jamie Brown ? I just called in to see the king"?

As the fleet came in, I could see crowds of people lining both sides of the harbour. There was music playing and the sound of cheering. The king himself was there, with a guard of blue-coated soldiers.

In the crowd, I could see somebody waving frantically. I looked again – it was Rob. But what on earth was he wearing? A red jacket, a red-and-yellow tie and a peaked cap... he looked ridiculous.

At least his shoulder must be better or he wouldn't be waving like that.

When we finally got ashore, I fought my way along the crowded quayside to find him. Ali was trying to do the same, but she got swallowed up by her own family. (It was easy to see they were her family. There were two fair-haired girls who looked very like her, if you could imagine Ali with long hair and wearing a dress.)

"Jamie! Oh, it's good to see you!" said Rob. "I didn't know if you were alive or dead!"

"I tried to send a message to you, but they said you'd left the hospital. Where did you get to – and what's *this* all about?" I flicked one finger, tipping Rob's cap back on his head.

"I'll tell you later. First, I want to know everything that happened. Did you see the guns being fired? Did you kill any Norsemen?"

He seemed to think that war was some kind of exciting game. It's not like that, I wanted to say – it's horrific. And all the heroes get killed.

I didn't have time to tell him about it, for Ali had arrived. "My mum says you're to come and have dinner with us," she said.

Rob looked anxious. "I'd better not be away from the castle for too long. See this uniform? I'm working as a royal messenger! Sir Kenneth gave me the job."

"Really? What do you have to do?" I asked.

"Take messages, of course. Mostly, it's inside the castle. But just now, I had to take a letter to the harbourmaster and I heard the fleet was coming in, so I waited to see you."

"Could Sir Kenneth get me a job too?" I said.

"Not this job. You have to be able to read. But I'll ask – there might be something else you could do."

"I don't care what it is, as long as I can earn my keep for a few months, and buy a boat that will take us home." I said this to see what Rob would say.

"Home?" He looked dismayed.

"Yes, home. To Insh More – remember it? We've done what we came here for."

"Maybe I won't go home again, ever. I like it here in Embra," he said.

Yes. That was what I was afraid of.

Because I didn't know what else to do, I went with Ali and her family. They owned a clothes shop on the wide, stony road leading up to the castle, and their home was three rooms above the shop. To me, the place looked small and cramped, but Ali said that it was good-sized by Embra standards. In the narrow closes that ran downhill between the shops, there were whole families living, eating and sleeping in one room.

"Don't go down the closes on your own at night," Ali warned me. "Not unless you want a knife in your back and all your money stolen."

"All what money?"

"Here, I can lend you some – I just got paid."

I took her money reluctantly. I didn't know how I would ever pay her back.

We had a good hot meal at Ali's place. When she realised that I had nowhere to go that night, she said, "Stay here. You'll have to sleep downstairs in the shop, though."

Her father didn't look too pleased about this, but Ali said, "Oh, go on, Dad, let him. He's not a thief. And he helped to save my life."

"All right. But he'll have to keep out of the way when the customers come in." He seemed to think my homespun clothes would look out of place in his shop.

I stayed there for three days, hoping to hear from Rob. If Sir Kenneth could find me a job, it would solve all my problems and maybe give me somewhere to live as well. But no word came. Probably, Rob had forgotten all about me.

At mealtimes, I sat and listened while Ali and her sisters discussed what I should do. I'd never even heard of some of the jobs they mentioned. I was amazed to hear that you could earn money by cleaning chimneys, baking bread, or collecting rubbish. On Insh More, people cleaned their own chimneys and baked their own bread – and as for rubbish, the pigs ate most of it.

"What is Jamie good at?" Ali's big sister asked her, just as if I wasn't there.

"Well... he can sail a boat all right. And hunt deer and catch fish," Ali said.

"Not much call for that kind of thing in Embra," said Ali's mother.

Strange to say, I'd worked that out for myself already. I wasn't stupid.

Ali's little sister said, "If he's good with boats, he could be a taxi-man, couldn't he?"

Everyone looked at her, surprised.

"Good thinking," said Ali, and the others agreed. I didn't mention that I had no idea what a taxi-man was.

After we'd eaten, Ali took me down to a slipway at the tip of the island. I'd hardly noticed before, but the king's ships were not the only things afloat around Embra. There were lots of smaller boats – rowing boats mostly – going to and fro.

"Most people don't have boats of their own," Ali explained, "so they pay for a taxi. The boatmen get quite good money. It's hard work though."

"You're forgetting something – I don't have a boat."

"You can row, though, can't you? I bet I can find you a job."

She was right, although she had to ask a lot of people first. I would have given up after the first few refusals, but Ali just went on asking.

At last she found a boat-owner who was looking for an oarsman. He took me out on the water. I soon proved to him that I could row all right, and bring the boat up to the jetty without bumping it.

"You'll do," he said. I'd already discovered that he didn't waste words. His name was Neil. He was elderly, brown and weather-beaten, with arms as strong as anchor ropes. He owned four boats and he said they were always busy.

"How much is the pay?" I asked him.

"Up to you – depends how hard you work. You keep half of what the customers pay. I get the other half."

That seemed a bit unfair, but then how would he know what the customers paid me? I decided to give him enough to keep him happy, and save up the rest towards a boat of my own.

When I explained that I was homeless, Neil said I could sleep in the boathouse if I wanted. He showed me it – a black-tarred wooden shed, with no door and gaps in the walls where the wind blew in.

"Better than nothing," said Neil.

True. It was better than nothing, but not much.

That night, as I lay restlessly on a pile of old ropes and nets, I listened to the water lapping. The tide was coming in. The same tide must be rising around Insh More, far away. And one day, I promised myself, the sea would take me back there... take me home.

11 On the Fiddle

Ali was right – it was hard work being a boatman. People were always in a hurry. Just because they were paying me, they expected me to row as if the Norsemen were after us.

The palms of my hands, which used to be as tough as leather, had got soft in the last few weeks. Soon, they were blistered from rowing. But in a few days, they began to toughen up again and Neil's other men, who had laughed at me to begin with, saw that I could actually do the job.

Tom, Craig and Ian, the other boatmen, played tricks on me now and then. One day, I was sent to a farm outside the city to fetch three sheep. "A country lad like you should be able to handle them all right," said Craig. "Just take plenty of rope with you."

Tom said, "Make sure they don't jump out of the boat."

I felt worried all the way over to the farm. But I needn't have bothered. The sheep were already dead, ready for delivery to an Embra butcher.

Because I was the new boy, I got the jobs nobody else wanted. One of them was a regular early-morning trip, taking workmen across to build the new aqueduct. This was a long, many-arched bridge, designed by the king's engineers. It would bring water from the hills outside the city, for Embra was always short of water.

I was putting my passengers ashore on the temporary pier beside the aqueduct, when one of the foremen called me over.

"Got an extra job for you, son," he said. "Good money – as long as you can keep your mouth shut."

He wanted me to take some pieces of cut stone to a small, outlying island. His men loaded them into my boat until it was low in the water. The foreman said I would get paid at the end of the journey.

"But, if you breathe a word of this to anybody, you'll be sorry," he warned me. "You'll end up going for a long swim – downwards. And never coming back up again."

"I won't tell," I promised. Of course I wouldn't. I didn't want my boss to know about anything extra I earned.

When I reached the island, two men with barrows were waiting by the pier, along with a man wearing the green uniform of the king's engineers. He paid me £5 – as much as I normally earned in a whole day. "There could be more where that came from, if you're reliable," he said.

Over his shoulder, I could see a half-built house where men were working. It looked to me as if materials and workmen had been diverted here from the aqueduct to build a house for somebody. Not for the king, surely... he already had a castle to live in. And why the secrecy?

The house, although it had no roof or windows yet, looked big and grand. It was the only building on the island. The master of the house – whoever he was – would feel like the ruler of his own private kingdom.

I wanted to find out more. But I kept my mouth shut. It would be stupid, maybe even dangerous, to ask questions.

I learned a lot in my first few days of work. I learned to ask for my money before I put people ashore, so that they couldn't run off without paying. I learned to avoid the shallows, where you could run aground at low tide... and, even more dangerous, the bridges, where people might tip rubbish over the side without looking. I soon began to know my way around Embra, or at least the areas close to the water line.

After I'd been working for several days, Rob tracked me down. He had asked Ali what had become of me, and she brought him down to the boathouse.

"I've found you a job at the castle," Rob told me.

"Oh, have you? It's a bit late now," I said coldly. "I could have starved to death if I'd been depending on you."

"Look, I'm sorry it took so long. But I had to wait for the right time to ask Sir Kenneth. I hardly ever see him – I mean, I'm only a messenger boy."

"Ali was more help than you were," I said. "She got me this job."

Ali looked pleased. She wasn't in uniform, I noticed. She said she was on shore leave while the *Dolphin* was being refitted.

It was the first time I had seen her in ordinary clothes, or what Embra people thought of as ordinary. (They seemed to like bright colours and strange, shiny-looking cloth. You could see them coming a mile off.)

"Don't you want to know what the job is?" asked Rob. I didn't answer, but he told me anyway. "Kitchen porter. You'd get food, clothes and lodging, plus £2 a week."

"£2 a *week*? You're joking. I earn more than that in a day! And I could never work in a kitchen. I can't cook."

"Oh, you wouldn't have to cook, there are chefs to do that. You'd just have to... I don't know, wash the pans, peel the potatoes, that kind of thing."

"Is that all you think I'm good for?" I said angrily. "Just because I can't read? Just because I'm not clever like you?"

"All right, it might not be a wonderful job, but it might lead to—"

"No thanks. I'd rather be a boatman. And I'll tell you something... you look stupid in that uniform. I wouldn't wear it for any money."

"At least it's clean," he said, annoyed. He was looking at my clothes, which hadn't been washed in a long time. "At least I don't smell of old fish."

"Oh, so as well as being stupid and ignorant, I stink?"

"I didn't mean—"

"Get out. Just get out and leave me alone."

After he'd gone, I felt terrible. I didn't want to quarrel with Rob. He was my best friend, even if our paths had gone in different directions lately.

There were good and bad things about my new job. The weather was the worst thing. If it poured with rain, we still had to work because people still needed to get around the city. I got soaked to the skin more than once, and I looked enviously at the hooded coats the other boatmen wore. They were made of sealskin, warm and waterproof.

"I could get you a coat like that, if you want," Tom offered.

"I can't afford it," I said. I had seen one like it on sale for over £200.

But Tom told me I could get one for a quarter of the price. He had a friend working in a tailor's shop, who could get things on the cheap.

It took me a couple of weeks, and some extra trips to the half-built house, to save up the £50. I gave the money to Tom and he came back with something wrapped up in a grubby-looking sack. My heart sank. I shouldn't have handed over all that money without seeing the coat.

But when I unwrapped it, the coat looked good. Slightly too big for me, but that didn't matter – I was still growing.

"Thanks, Tom! And say thank you to your friend for me. It's really good of him."

I saw Tom give Craig a sly grin.

"What's the matter? Is there something wrong with the coat?" I demanded.

"No, no. It's fine. It looks good on you."

In the end, I found out that Tom's friend had stolen the coat from the shop where he worked. "He does that every now and then," said Tom. "Not too often, in case he gets found out. And why shouldn't he? His boss hardly pays him enough to live on."

Craig said, "You'll soon learn, country boy. Everybody in Embra's on the fiddle, one way or another."

"On the fiddle?" To me, the fiddle meant the old violin that Rob's uncle brought out on special occasions such as weddings. Obviously, it meant something different here.

"He means on the make," Tom explained. "Finding ways to get a bit more money than you get paid."

"Does that not happen on your island, country boy?" asked Craig.

"Well, no."

"Because they haven't invented money there yet," said Ian. "They buy things using sheepskins, and hens, and dead fish."

The others laughed, and I felt my face turn red.

"We do have money," I said. "But people are honest because... well, because everybody knows everybody else. If you cheated somebody, you'd soon get found out."

"Then I'm glad I live in the city," said Tom.

"Jamie's learning the city ways, though," said Craig, and he winked at me. "The boss doesn't get anything like half of what you earn, does he, country boy?"

Had Craig been spying on me? "That's not true," I said, alarmed.

"Oh, come on. You could never afford that coat if you weren't getting a bit extra here and there," said Ian.

"Don't worry," said Tom. "We all do it. As long as we don't keep hold of too much money, Neil lets us get away with it. What else can he do?"

"He can sack you," said Craig. "And he will, if you get too greedy, Jamie-boy. Be warned. There are dozens of other lads who'd jump at the chance to do this job."

12 Stormy weather

I went to a boatbuilder's yard to find out how much it would cost to buy a sailing boat. What I had in mind was nothing grand - just a small fishing-boat with a single mast and sail. That was the type of boat that had started us on our journey to Embra.

I was shocked to find that even the cheapest one would cost hundreds of pounds. I would have to save up for months - all through the winter probably. And Tom told me that, when stormy weather came, there would be days and days when we couldn't earn a penny.

The weather has changed since the Old Times, or so people say. It's not as cold as it used to be, but storms are more violent, and they happen more often.

At home on Insh More, we would fasten the shutters and stay indoors until the storm blew over. In Embra, the streets emptied when the weather got really bad, and nobody needed boatmen - luckily for us.

One stormy day, I was sitting in the boathouse all by myself. The other boatmen hadn't even bothered to turn up for work; they'd stayed at home, keeping warm. I was feeling cold and lonely. The wind howled through the gaps in the wooden walls, and rain rattled on the roof and dripped through the holes in it.

"Anybody there?" someone shouted from outside.

Oh, no. Surely it wasn't a customer! Maybe if I didn't answer, they would go away.

But it was Ali. She came in through the open front of the boathouse, looking wet and wind-blown.

"Rob's here too," she said. "Are you still speaking to him?"

When I nodded, she shouted, "Come in, Rob. I told you it would be all right."

I hadn't seen him since our quarrel, two weeks ago. The quarrel seemed silly now. A few times I'd almost gone up to the castle looking for Rob, but each time I lost my nerve. What if he didn't want to know me any more?

Suddenly, I realised that Rob might have felt the same about me... afraid I would reject him... afraid that *I* didn't want to know *him* any more.

"Come in, Rob," I shouted. "Or do you like standing in the rain? If so, don't worry. It's raining in here too."

"Yes," said Ali. "This ceiling's got more holes in it than a sieve."

Rob came in, looking even wetter than Ali. Neither of us said anything about our last meeting, but soon it felt as if the quarrel had never happened. Things were back as they used to be, including Ali getting bossy.

"You can't go on living here, Jamie," she told me. "Not through the winter."

She told me she'd heard of a room to rent in a close off the High Street. "It's quite small and it's about six floors up, but at least you'd be dry. It costs £5 a week."

"What?"

"That's Embra prices for you. Actually, it's pretty cheap – nobody wants to live there. But why don't you have a look at the room before you decide? Look, come round to our place for dinner. You look like you need a good hot meal."

It was the meal that persuaded me. After we'd eaten, Ali led us down the close – a shadow-filled alley hardly wide enough for two people to pass each other. Tall houses towered up on both sides, cutting out the light. The cobblestones were slippery underfoot, and the Embra smell (smoke, rotting food and open drains) seemed worse than usual. But the high buildings sheltered us from the wind and the rain.

The landlord was a mean-faced old man who lived on the ground floor of his building. He led us up a long staircase with countless doors leading off it. Through the thin walls, I could hear children shouting, a baby crying, a drunken argument... At least this place wouldn't feel as lonely as the boathouse.

The room was tiny. It held a bed, a table and chair, and a metal stove – nothing else. I would have to use an outside toilet shared by everybody else in the building.

The room didn't look too clean either and the ceiling was grey with cobwebs.

But in the end, I decided to take it. As Ali had said, I couldn't spend the whole winter in that leaky shed.

Later, Ali told me that the room was cheap because nobody seemed to stay there for long.

"Why not?"

"Some daft nonsense about an old lady that died there. People must have died in every room in that building over the years, so why worry? I tell you one thing you should worry about, though – your money. Don't keep your savings in that place."

So I went on hiding my money under a loose board in the boathouse.

A couple of days later, I found out more about the old lady who had died in my room. I got talking to my neighbour across the landing, a big fat woman with about eight children. She told me that the old lady had no family and nobody to miss her so that, when she died, it was weeks before anyone noticed.

"After a while, I thought, *it's a long time since I've seen old Morag*," she explained. "And, when the landlord opened up the door, he found she'd been dead for ages. The rats had eaten most of her, down to the bones."

I must have looked shocked. This would never have happened at home. Old people were better looked after there.

The woman said, "Don't blame me! I didn't have time to keep an eye on her! I've got enough on my plate. And she was a bad-tempered old biddy, forever yelling at my kids. If she didn't have any friends, it was her own fault." She slammed the door.

When I told Ali about this, she said, "That's Embra for you. Everybody looks after themselves. They don't have time to think about other people."

I was liking Embra less and less. But I was stuck here, at least for the winter.

One day, on my way home from work, I saw a familiar figure limping along the High Street. I hurried to catch up with him.

"Graham! Hi there!"

"Jamie... what are you doing still here? I thought you'd have set off home ages ago."

I told him about my struggle to save up for a boat. He told me that he'd been sacked from the radio project. Now he was working in the public library, making copies of books. "It's pretty dull compared with what I was doing before. But at least it's a job."

I didn't know what he meant by *public library*, so he showed me the place. It was in a building on the High

Street - a big room with high walls and tall rows of shelves. He'd told me it was full of books but, when I looked round, I couldn't see any.

"Where are all these books, then?"

He laughed and the woman in charge gave him a disapproving look. It seemed we were meant to speak in whispers, so that we didn't disturb the people who had come to read. There were only a few of them, and some looked like street beggars who were just there to get out of the cold.

"This is a book," Graham whispered, lifting something from a rack on the wall. It looked to me like a big roll of cloth but, when he began to unroll it, I saw that there was writing all over one side of it. "Or maybe I should call it a copy of a book: *Guinness World Records 2015*. The original book is very old and fragile. It's in the castle library, for safe keeping."

"Why doesn't this look more like a book, though?"

"We don't know yet how the Ancestors made their books. They must have had some kind of machine, because all the letters are exactly the same - but we can only guess what it looked like. Maybe one day, we'll find a book on how to make books. At the moment, we can only make copies by hand. Look, this is the one I'm working on."

He led me to a table under a window. A writing roll was spread out, partly written-on and partly blank. And beside it was a book from the Old Times. I stared at it.

I would have known that book anywhere. I'd carried it all the way from the far north-west, where I had found it in an abandoned house.

"That's *my* book," I said. "The one I gave to the king. Why is it here?"

13 Robbers

"**Y**our book is here to be copied out, on the king's orders," said Graham. "When I've finished, the original book will be stored safely at the castle, but the copy will be here for anybody who wants to read it."

I was pleased to hear that. I wondered if Rob knew about this library place – he would be very interested.

"It's a strange kind of book," Graham said. "Not like anything I've read before."

"How do you mean?"

"Well, it's obviously quite old. It would have been old even in the time of the Ancestors. It mentions a great flood – far worse than the rising seas in the Ancestors' time. The whole earth was underwater. That flood, it says, was sent as a punishment because there was so much evil in the world."

"There was evil in the time of the Ancestors too," I said. "Why didn't the sea drown *them*?"

"The book says that God promised there would never be such terrible flooding again."

"This God – it's all just a story, isn't it? Or do you really think there is a God?"

Graham said, "I don't know. Maybe God exists, but everybody's forgotten about him. They don't want to follow his rules. They want to please themselves. And so the world is still full of evil... wars and thieving and greed and hatred and envy... I can't help thinking that, if everybody lived by this book, the world would be a better place."

"Maybe," I said.

"Look, here are some of the commands in the book. I was writing them out this morning."

He read me a list. Don't steal; don't tell lies; don't desire the things that belong to other people – that sort of stuff. I can't remember them all, but there was one that went into my heart like an arrow. *Do not murder.*

I had tried to forget the Norseman I had killed. The memories of the battle were so bad that, whenever they came to mind, I pushed them away and thought of something else. But suddenly, I could picture him quite clearly – a boy not much older than me, standing on a hillside in the sun. He had no idea that I was about to snuff out his life like a half-used candle.

Was that murder? He was my enemy – surely I was meant to kill him! Even though he hadn't done anything to hurt me... hadn't even seen me.

Granny used to say that anyone who was murdered would come back to haunt their killer. Maybe that was why I kept having dreams about the battle, waking up terrified and covered in sweat. The Norseman was haunting me. He would never leave me in peace.

The woman at the desk rang a little bell. "We're closing now," she called out.

The readers rolled up their books. The beggars gathered up their few belongings. I said goodbye to Graham, promising to come back and see him now that I knew where he worked. Then I went out into the gathering darkness.

I bought a loaf of bread and some cheese for my supper. But I didn't go back to my room straight away. I didn't want to sit there all alone, thinking about death, in the place where the old woman had lain dead for so long. And I was afraid of going to sleep, falling helpless into that dream.

So I walked around the streets for a while. In spite of the crowd all around me, I felt quite lonely. But the crowd was thinning now as the shops closed for the night. And it was getting cold. I would have to go home.

Compared to the lighted High Street, the mouth of the close looked very dark. Further down, there would be a bit of lamplight from windows, but the first part was like a dark tunnel under the High Street buildings. I kept one hand on the side wall, to guide me.

My hand came to a gap in the wall - a doorway or something. I stepped forward, reaching out for the other side of it. But, instead of cold stone, my fingers touched something warm and alive.

Someone was standing in the doorway, silent and motionless... waiting?

My hand leapt away. Without having time even to think, I started running. Why hadn't I remembered Ali's warning? "*Don't go down the closes on your own at night unless you want a knife in your back...*"

My feet slipped on the greasy cobblestones. I almost fell. Struggling up again, I felt strong arms grab hold of me. I cried out, fighting to get away and somebody swore at me.

Then something heavy struck my head; it struck me so hard that it made me dizzy. I was falling again; I couldn't help myself...

"Careful. If you get blood on that coat, I'll kill you," a voice said. A voice I knew?

Another jolt of pain hit my skull. That's all I remember.

I heard someone groan. I tried to move, and stopped. It felt as if red-hot metal was boring into my skull.

Slowly I realised where I was... lying in a gutter in an Embra close. The groaning sound came again. I found that it was coming from my own throat.

I couldn't get up. I couldn't even lift my head to look up when I heard footsteps coming closer. Two pairs of feet stopped, not far from my face.

"Dear me. What a state to get into!" said a lady's voice.

"Maybe this will teach him not to drink so much," said her friend.

They walked around me and went away.

I don't know how long I lay there, shivering with cold – the robbers had taken my coat. One or two other people went past without stopping. A barefooted child paused for a moment, then snatched up my loaf of bread and ran away.

I made another effort to get up. But the dizzy feeling came over me again, and I was sick. Once again I collapsed on the ground.

I thought I was going to die there – surrounded by thousands of people, yet all alone. The thought terrified me. I didn't want to die... didn't want to be snuffed out like a candle and left in the dark...

Oh, God, if there is a God – please help me! Don't let me die here in the gutter!

"What happen to you?" said a voice.

Somebody was bending over to look at me. I could see him dimly in the light from the windows above. A big man, fair-haired and bearded, he wore a leather jacket and breeches like the Norsemen wore.

A Norseman! Or the ghost of one! I screamed in terror.

"Do not fear. I will not hurt you," he said, touching my arm. "You fall down? You bleed much, very much."

"Robbers attacked me," I gasped. The touch of his hand had proved that the man was real, not a ghost. All the same, I was very scared.

"Whassamatter?" came another voice, slurred with drink. A filthy, unshaven face came into view – the eyes bloodshot, the breath stinking of whisky. He looked like an Embra beggar-man.

The first man said, "This boy is hit by robbers. He needs help."

"Annie will help. Get him to Annie's place," said the beggar.

"Where is that place?"

"Just down the hill. Not far. Up you get, laddie."

Between them, the two men somehow managed to get me off the ground. Then we began to stagger down the close, with the Norseman and the beggar holding me up. I had no idea where they were taking me.

At last, we stopped outside a door. The beggar thumped on it and shouted, "Annie! Annie! Open up! Here's another stray dog for you."

The door opened. Inside, there was light, and warmth, and the smell of cooking.

"Come in, and welcome," said a woman's voice.

"I must go now," said the Norseman. "The boy is safe here?"

"He'll be fine. Annie will take care of him. Careful, sonny – try and not fall over the doorstep."

14 Annie's place

Annie was a small, round-faced, smiling lady, with grey hair pulled back in a bun. She couldn't have been kinder to me if I'd been her own grandson.

She made me sit down. Gently, she examined my wounds and cleaned them up. She took off my shirt, which was stained with blood and vomit, and went to find a clean one – all this before she knew anything about me.

The dizziness was fading; I began to look around. I was in a huge room, dimly lit by candles here and there. The roof was so high that it was hidden in darkness. The Great Hall at the castle might look like this, if it was invaded by beggars.

The place was crowded with people, all poor and hungry-looking. They shuffled forward in a long queue towards a table where two women were dishing out food.

What on earth was this place? I would have asked the man who'd helped me, but he had gone to join the food queue. I had no desire to eat – my head was still thumping with pain.

Annie came bustling back with some clean clothes and a blanket.

"Stay the night here," she said. "Then I can keep an eye on that head of yours. If need be, we'll take you to the hospital tomorrow."

"Hospital!" I said, alarmed. I knew from Rob's hospital visit that it would cost money. "I don't have any cash on me. The robbers took it."

Annie smiled at me. "Don't you worry. We've got a bit put aside for times like this. Now, tell me what your name is, and where you're from. You don't sound to me like an Embra boy."

I told her a bit of my story. She was a good listener. She made me feel as if I was the only person in the world who mattered to her. As if I was part of her family... even though I was a complete stranger.

"I bet *you're* not from Embra either," I said to her.

"What makes you say that?"

"Because you're nice. Because you care about people." I looked around the big room. "Does this place belong to you?"

"No. It's a church. It was built in the Old Times as a place for people to come and pray. So I suppose, if it belongs to anybody, it belongs to God."

"Doesn't God mind that all these beggars have taken over his house?" I asked.

"Oh, no. He wants them to be here," she said quite seriously. "He showed me this place, years ago, when I was looking for a base to work from. I was praying about it all the time as I walked around Embra. One day, I came down the close and noticed the door there, with the sign of the cross above it carved in stone. And I felt God was telling me: 'Look, here you are.'"

This was a bit weird. I'd never heard anyone who claimed that God had spoken to them. I would have laughed at Annie, but she had been kind to me. So I kept silent.

"You think I'm some kind of mad woman?" she said.

"Well... "

"A lot of people would agree with you," she said cheerfully. "I spent years training as a doctor. I could be using my skills to make money and live in luxury. But I would rather help the people who can't afford to visit doctors and who can't even afford to buy food half the time."

Somebody was calling her name. She got up slowly, as if she was tired.

"Sleep over there in the corner, Jamie," she told me. "I'll be here if you need me."

It wasn't a good night's sleep. The pain in my head kept waking me. Annie must have heard me tossing and turning; she gave me some bitter-tasting medicine to drink, and said a prayer for me. After that, I slept.

When I awoke, the big room was almost empty. Sunlight came streaming in through a strange-looking window that turned the light into different colours – purple, green and gold. The room seemed much quieter than the night before. Maybe all the beggars were out at their work.

I could hear the murmur of voices. Sitting up carefully – this made my head ache again – I saw Annie with a group of children. She had a book open on her knee and she was reading aloud.

I wondered why she kept a book in a place like this. Books were valuable – even the beggars must know that. It could easily get stolen.

When Annie saw me trying to get up, she came hurrying over. She called for a woman to help her and, between them, they got me up on my feet. I walked a few steps and then had to sit down again.

It was clear that I couldn't go back to work yet. But I was worried that, if I didn't turn up, Neil would take on somebody else to do my job. Annie put my mind at rest by sending two of the children to find him and tell him what had happened.

That night, when I saw the man who had helped me, I tried to thank him. But he'd been drinking again and had no idea what I was talking about.

I spent several days at Annie's place, getting my strength back. My first impressions of her had been quite accurate. She was very nice; she welcomed everyone, even the smelliest old tramp. She was also crazy.

"Where does the money come from to feed all these people?" I asked her one evening. She was standing behind me in the food queue, holding the arm of a blind woman.

"God sends it." At the look on my face, she laughed. "Jamie thinks I'm mad, Ellen. But it's true, isn't it? Whenever we're about to run out of money, we pray. And God touches people's hearts, and they give to us – not always the rich people either. Sometimes, it's the poorest people who give us a few pennies. Or a baker brings us some loaves he couldn't sell."

The blind woman said to me, "I've been coming here for years now, and never been sent away hungry. Annie never lets us down."

"You mean, *God* never lets us down," said Annie.

After everyone had eaten, Annie read aloud from that book of hers. It interested me because it was a bit like my own book, but the words were simpler.

"Jesus said, 'God knows everything about you. He even knows how many hairs are on your head! And he loves you. He loves everything that he made. Sparrows are sold for just a few pennies, but God cares for all of them. And you are worth much more than many sparrows. So don't be afraid... God will take care of you.'"

I longed to believe this, but I couldn't. If God knew so much about me, he must know about the bad things I'd done. He must hate me. Maybe he took care of good, kind people like Annie... not me though.

Really? What about when you prayed for help, and the Norseman and the beggar came along?

This thought almost made me laugh out loud. A Norseman and a beggar! Could they really be answers to a prayer?

When I asked, Annie let me have a look at the book. I turned the pages carefully so as not to tear them. There were pictures here and there – I'd never seen a book with pictures in it. Maybe they had once been brightly-coloured, but they were old and faded now.

I said, "What's the name of this book?"

"*Bible Stories for Children*. It's been passed down through my family for generations. I believe it's a child's version of a much longer book, but that must have been lost long ago. Maybe it never existed."

"It did exist," I said. "It still does. It's being copied out in the public library."

"What?"

When I told her all about the book, she got very excited. Next day, she went off to the library as soon as she could. She came back even more excited.

"It's amazing! I've seen the complete book – and there's so much more to it than in my storybook!"

"Graham let you look at it, then?"

"Yes, I read quite a bit when he took a break from writing. And he says I can read the library copy as much as I want. Or I can even make my own copy." She sighed with longing. "That would be wonderful!"

"I can't understand all this fuss over a book," I couldn't help saying.

Annie said, "It's full of the words of God. All about good and evil – life and death."

The next day, I felt well enough to go back to work. I thanked Annie and her friends, wishing I had some money on me to pay for my keep.

My boss was quite grumpy when I arrived at the boathouse.

"Decided to show up, then?" he said. "About time. We need you. That Tom lad upped and left yesterday. Said he's bought a boat of his own."

"Oh, has he? I wonder where he got the money," I said.

I hadn't forgotten the night when I was attacked. I had thought I knew the voice of the attacker. Surely it hadn't been Tom?

But I could be wrong about the voice. Any man with an Embra accent might sound like Tom, or Craig, or Ian. And a stolen sealskin coat wouldn't be worth enough to buy a boat – not even a rowing boat. Luckily, I hadn't been carrying too much cash that night. Most of my money was hidden in the boathouse.

Or was it? Suddenly, a terrible fear gripped me...

I ran to the back of the boathouse. The loose board was still in place, but when I moved it aside, my heart sank.

The hiding place was empty. All my money was gone.

15 Lost instructions

"How much got taken?" asked Rob.

"I don't know exactly. It must have been over £100. I just used to put the money in quickly and cover it up. I couldn't sit there counting it in case somebody saw me."

"Somebody did see you though," said Ali. "Was it the same guy that stole your coat?"

"I bet it was," I said. "If I find him, I'll kill him."

Tom – for it was Tom I was thinking of – was a grown man. If it came to a fight, I would probably be the one who got killed. But I was too angry to think clearly.

A hundred pounds! Weeks and weeks it had taken me to save up that much. And now the winter was coming on, with cold weather when I would freeze without my coat, and storms when I couldn't work at all.

It was no use planning to go home in the spring. I still wouldn't have a boat by then. I would have to keep on working... keep on living in this city that I hated.

"Did you say the thief bought his own taxi-boat?" said Rob. "Then he shouldn't be too hard to track down. You're bound to cross paths with him sooner or later."

"You could follow him, and find out where he keeps the boat, and then nick it," said Ali.

"Don't be stupid," I said. "What would I do with a rowing boat? I can't row all the way to Insh More!"

"You could sell it and get your money back."

"That's not such a bad idea," I said.

Rob, Ali and I were in a café. We tried to meet up there once a week on Rob's day off, just to make sure we kept in touch. It was a crowded, noisy place in a side street not far from the castle.

Suddenly, the room fell silent. Everyone was looking towards the door, at two men who had just come in. Two tall, fair-haired men in jackets of leather. Two Norsemen?

They didn't seem to notice the silence in the room, or the hostile looks they were getting. But then the café owner came out from behind his table and walked up to them.

"Sorry, we're full," he said.

It was true the café was crowded, but it was also clear that he didn't want to serve the two foreigners. He took them each by the arm and guided them towards the door. When he closed it behind them, a few people cheered.

"Well done!"

"Filthy Norsemen! Kick them out!"

I said to Rob, "Why are those Norsemen still in Embra?"

"They're waiting for their ship to be mended. Or that's the story."

"If you ask me," said Ali, "their ship could have been fixed ages ago. But the king doesn't want them to leave."

"He wants to marry the Norse woman, Valda," said Rob. "Where have you been for the last month, Jamie? You must have heard the gossip."

Ali said, "And what about the other bit of gossip – that Sir Kenneth won't agree to the marriage?"

"Surely the king can marry anyone he likes," I said.

"Not until he's 21," said Rob. "He was just 14 – too young to be ruling the country – when his father was about to die. So old King James chose Sir Kenneth to be his guardian and guide him in making decisions. It worked out fine... until now."

"But in a couple of weeks, King Andrew will have his 21st birthday," said Ali. "Then he can decide things for himself. He can kick Sir Kenneth out if he wants to."

"And marry Valda," said Rob.

"Yes, if she'll have him," Ali said. "If I was her, I'd try not to seem too keen. Make him worry. Make him sweat a bit."

I wasn't very interested in any of this. My mind had gone back to the man who'd helped me when I was attacked.

What had he been doing down that close at night? Visiting a gambling den, maybe, or looking for a woman. Or spying out the city, finding places where invaders might land. (At high tide, the sea came right up to the foot of the close.)

I couldn't get rid of the fear of Norsemen. Norsemen were our enemies. And yet one of them had helped me; maybe he had saved my life... It was all very puzzling.

I bought myself a thick, dark cloak to wear at work. It wasn't nearly as waterproof as the sealskin coat, but at least it was warm. And it might help to disguise me if I saw Tom.

When I asked the other boatmen if they knew where he'd gone, Craig said he was probably based on one of the other islands, where there wasn't so much competition for passengers. I tried to look out for him whenever I was on the water. But there were so many boats and, from a distance, all the boatmen looked alike.

I didn't tell the other men about the missing money. I didn't want to see their pitying smiles. They thought I was a know-nothing country boy who didn't understand city life. *They* would never have been stupid enough to hide £100 in a boathouse.

Ali told me I could keep my money in her father's safe, which was a sort of secret cupboard made of thick metal, with a lock and key. So, every day, I took some of my earnings to his shop. He wrote down how much I'd given him, but I also kept a careful total in my head. I had learned the first lesson of city life – don't trust anybody.

The weather was turning colder and the nights getting longer. Then came the first of the winter storms, which lasted for two days. Feeling bored because I had nothing to do, I went to see Graham at the library.

He was still working his way through my book. His written copy had already filled three of the library rolls, and he was on his fourth one.

"You must be tired of it," I said.

He shook his fingers, which had been cramped around the pen. "Tired of writing – yes," he said. "But not tired of the book. It's an astonishing book, you know. I've never read anything like it."

"Read me a bit," I said.

"*If anyone hits you on one cheek, let him hit the other one too; if someone takes your coat, let him have your shirt as well,*" Graham read.

"What? Are you kidding me? It doesn't really say that."

"Yes, it does. And what about this? *Love your enemies and do good to them; lend and expect nothing back. You will then have a great reward, and you will be sons of the Most High God. For he is good to the ungrateful and the wicked.*"

I turned this over in my mind. *God is good to the ungrateful and the wicked.* Even to a murderer? Even to someone like me?

"Do you believe what the book says?" I asked Graham.

"I'd like to. I'd like to think there really is a God who loves us. And, when you look around at the world, it's all such a mess. People fighting wars, stealing, hating each other... the rich getting richer, the poor getting poorer... it's like we've lost the instructions."

"What do you mean – lost the instructions?"

"Remember when I couldn't fix the radio, because I lost that piece of paper? This book has been lost for a long, long time. Most people have forgotten what it says. So, when things go wrong, we don't know how to fix them."

"You really think this book could put right everything that's wrong with the world."

"Not the book itself. But, if people were to read it and do what it says... "

I laughed. "You'd better get back to work then, Graham. If everybody is to read it, we're going to need thousands of copies."

He sighed and picked up his pen.

16 Knife in hand

It was weird that a book written long ago could speak to me so clearly. Twice, now, words from the book had struck home. "*If someone takes your coat...*" That might have been written just for me.

Of course, if the robbers had wanted my shirt, they'd have taken it, and I wouldn't have been able to stop them. That wasn't the point. I knew what the words meant: don't get angry if somebody does wrong to you. Don't try to hit back.

But why shouldn't I get angry? The thieves had attacked me and hurt me. They'd taken my belongings. *Anybody* would be angry. It was only natural. Why should I care about some words from an old book?

There was only one person I could talk to about this – Annie. I went to see her, but she wasn't there. Her friends said she was visiting someone in the hospital.

I went to meet up with Rob and Ali. Ali was back in uniform because her shore leave was coming to an end. The *Dolphin* was being made ready for the king's birthday. The whole city, in fact, was being made ready. There would be a day of feasting and celebration, with a 21-gun salute, and a procession, and fireworks at night.

"And then, I bet, the king will ask that Norse woman to marry him," said Ali.

"You sound like you don't think it's a good idea," said Rob. "Why?"

"Because he might end up with a rebellion on his hands. Most Embra people hate the Norsemen."

"Don't you hate them?" I asked Rob.

"Not Harald Haraldson and his people – no. I'm sure they're not enemies or spies. Didn't one of them help you when you got attacked?"

"Yes," I admitted. "But I still don't feel as if I trust them."

"Sir Kenneth would agree with you," said Rob. "He's told us to keep a careful eye on them. We have to report to him if we see them doing anything suspicious."

Work on the aqueduct had stopped for the winter; there were no more journeys to the mysterious house on the island. And people were making fewer trips, staying at home when they could.

This meant I had far less money coming in. Often, after paying for my room and my food, I had nothing left over.

I was still keeping a lookout for Tom. If I could find him, there might be some way of getting my money back – even if I had to steal his boat. A couple of times, I thought I saw him, but each time I was mistaken.

One day, I took a shoemaker to the leather tannery. It was on Arthur's Isle, the biggest of the Embra islands.

Hardly anyone lived there, maybe because the land was so steep and rocky. There were rows of strange machines all along the upper slopes – wind turbines, they were called. Graham had told me that they made power to light up the High Street and the castle at night.

That afternoon, there was hardly enough wind to stir the blades of the turbines. The air felt cold and damp, and a mist was creeping in from the sea, getting thicker all the time. The shoemaker looked anxious as I rowed him homewards.

"Don't worry," I told him. "We won't get lost. I know Embra like the back of my hand."

Another boat slipped across our wake. Out of habit, I looked to see who was rowing it. Then I looked again. It was Tom.

He hadn't seen me. I quickly turned away and pulled up the hood of my cloak. I was determined to follow him – it might be ages before I saw him again.

I took my passenger to the nearest jetty, which wasn't even close to where he wanted to go. When he protested, I took out my knife. I'd bought it soon after I was attacked, and it had already come in useful a few times.

"Get out," I told him. "Right now."

The man hurriedly scrambled out, and I threw his parcels onto the jetty.

"I'll report you!" he shouted. But already, I was rowing away.

Which way had Tom gone? It had looked as if he was heading south-eastwards, out of the city. Now the mist had swallowed him up.

A huge shape loomed through the mist – the aqueduct. It was silent and deserted. I rowed on, starting to lose hope. Tom could have changed direction; he could be anywhere by now.

But the mist lifted just for a moment or two, and I saw another boat. It must be him. There was hardly anyone else out on the water, for it was getting dark by now.

That was strange. The boat was close to an island: the island with the grand, half-built house. I wondered why anyone would want to go there at nightfall.

I shipped my oars and let the boat drift, listening. Voices came to me through the fog.

"You will wait here for us, boatman?"

"Yes, sir. Are you going to be long?"

"I do not know. I am here to meet someone. He will come very soon, I think."

I hadn't spared any attention for Tom's passenger. But now I thought he sounded like a Norseman. What was he doing here? If only he would go away and give me the chance to creep up on Tom...

Maybe I should try to land. But not at the jetty – Tom would see me coming. I wouldn't be able to surprise him and, if he was ready for me, I wouldn't have a chance against him, even with my knife.

As quietly as possible, I rowed along the shore of the island until I found a place to land. I tied the boat to a rock and crept back towards the jetty.

Another boat had arrived. I watched from the shelter of some rocks as two men got out of it. One of them lit a lantern, and I gasped with surprise, for the light shone on a face I knew – Sir Kenneth, the king's chief adviser.

In a low voice, he talked to the man who had got out of Tom's boat. I recognised him too: Harald Haraldson, the Norse leader. The whole thing had a secretive look about it, especially when Sir Kenneth led the other two up the path towards the empty house.

What was going on? Sir Kenneth didn't trust the Norsemen, so why was he meeting their leader here in secret?

I didn't spend too much time wondering about this. I had something more important on my mind – getting my money back.

Tom had been left behind at the jetty. I saw his dark shape, sitting on a rock with his back to me. He was all alone. I would never have another chance like this!

Knife in hand, I crept towards him. If I took him by surprise and got my knife to his throat, he would be in my power. He'd have to tell me the truth about my coat and my money.

And then what?

A dark mist of fury seemed to rise up in front of me. I thought of how the robbers hadn't cared about hurting me, except to worry about getting blood on my coat.

I would kill him. It would be easy. Kill him and steal his boat and get away into the darkness.

17 Secrets

Maybe my anger made me careless. Maybe it's impossible to walk silently over a stony beach. Anyway, Tom heard me.

Before I reached him, he was up on his feet, and I saw the gleam of metal - he had a knife too.

"Who's there?" he hissed. "What do you want?"

"I want my money! Give it back or I'll kill you!"

"What money?" He sounded genuinely surprised. "Look, whoever you are, you've got the wrong man. I don't know what you're talking about."

"My money that you stole from the boathouse! My money that you bought your boat with!"

"Jamie!" Now he sounded even more amazed. "What are you doing here? I warn you, it's not a good place to be right now. If Sir Kenneth sees you... "

"Don't try and pretend you don't know what I'm talking about," I said furiously. "My money!"

"Calm down, son," he said, backing away. "I know you hid some money at the boathouse. We all knew - Craig and Ian and me - and Craig used to say you deserved to lose it if you couldn't look after it. But I never took it, Jamie; I swear it."

I almost believed him. Then I remembered what a good actor he was. Often, with a completely straight face, he had tricked me into doing something stupid.

"If you didn't take it, how did you get the money for your boat?" I asked.

"You think you're the only one that can save up money? I've been saving for years, son. I didn't want to work for Neil all my life! But now I don't have to - I can be my own boss. And I've got a friend working at the castle. He often gets me jobs like this one. Private work for Sir Kenneth... double pay."

I didn't say anything because I was thinking fast. If Craig and Ian knew about my money too, either of them could have taken it. And either of them - or both - could have attacked me in the close. Tom might be quite innocent.

"Put that knife down," Tom said. "You're making me nervous, waving it about like that."

I held onto the knife. "You think it could have been Craig or Ian that robbed me, then?"

"Maybe. Craig - well, you know him, he'd bet on anything, and he's always losing. He owes people a lot of money. I wouldn't put it past him to steal from you. But listen, Jamie... as I said, you shouldn't be here."

"Why not?"

Tom hesitated. "Sir Kenneth wouldn't like it."

"Wouldn't like what? Wouldn't like people knowing he met up with the Norse leader in secret?"

"Shhhh."

Suddenly, I realised something. "So it's Sir Kenneth that owns this house! I always wondered who it belonged to."

Just for a moment, I looked towards the house. It was a mistake. In that moment, Tom leaped forward and grabbed my wrist. His strong fingers prised the knife out of my hand. Then he threw it far out into the darkness – I heard it splash into the water.

"Jamie, I could kill you if I wanted." His voice was harsh. "And I'm telling you – come after me again and you'll be sorry."

"Let go of me!"

"Okay." He shoved me so hard that I almost fell over. "Now get out of here before Sir Kenneth comes back."

I stumbled away, feeling furious with myself. I had really messed things up. I'd lost my knife, which had cost me quite a bit of money. And I still didn't know who had robbed me. Everything Tom had said could be lies.

Before I'd gone very far, though, something else was bothering me. Sir Kenneth and the Norse leader were here, meeting in secret. What was that all about? Were they plotting against King Andrew?

My feet slowed and then stopped. I couldn't leave the island without at least trying to find out what was going on.

I climbed up over the rocks, heading for the house. The darkness and the mist would hide me, but I would have to be very quiet.

Through the trees, I saw the glow of lamplight. I crept closer. Now I could hear voices from inside the house, which was still unfinished, with no doors and no glass in the windows. I threaded my way between sand-heaps and piles of rubble.

Soon I was crouching down beneath the window sill. I could hear almost every word the men were saying.

"Ah, so you agree with me, Harald?" Sir Kenneth said. "You're not in favour of the marriage?"

"I think that if Valda marry your king, she may be happy for a little while. But soon, she will be very lonely, here in this city where everyone hates our people. I think it is better if she marry the son of my friend, Sir John of Durham. This is what we planned long ago."

Sir Kenneth said, "And long ago, it was planned that King Andrew should marry Lady Isobel, my niece. That was the wish of his father before he died."

I felt quite sorry for Valda and King Andrew. Where I came from, people could marry whoever they wanted, without their families interfering.

"And it is your wish too?" Harald said. "Your niece marries the king and you will still be powerful in Embra."

Sir Kenneth laughed. "Whatever happens, I'll still be powerful. Make no mistake about that."

Another voice said something I couldn't hear. It must be the man who had arrived in the boat with Sir Kenneth. I had no idea who he might be. He wasn't just a boatman or he wouldn't have been included in this meeting.

"Valda is my daughter," Harald said. "She will obey me. And I think that, if we are far away from here, she will soon forget about King Andrew. But how can we go away? Without our ship, we are prisoners in Embra."

"Your ship is ready," said Sir Kenneth. "It could have been ready weeks ago, but the king ordered the work to go as slowly as possible. He wanted to keep you here until his birthday."

"His birthday is tomorrow, yes?"

"That's right. Tomorrow, he'll be 21 years old. Then he plans to ask you formally for Valda's hand in marriage. I've persuaded him at least to wait until after the birthday celebrations – half of Embra will be drunk and there could easily be trouble when the news is known. But I can't stop him from asking."

"And if I say no?"

"That wouldn't be a wise move. The king is used to getting his own way. Do you understand me? On the surface he seems kind and friendly but, if people disobey him, he can be quite ruthless."

That's a lie! I wanted to shout. *King Andrew isn't like that at all!*

"What do you mean?" asked Harald.

"I mean he'd get you out of the way and marry her anyway."

"Get me out of the way?" Harald said. "Do you mean he will kill me?"

"Exactly. But I don't want that to happen. I can help you escape from Embra – you and all your people."

"Tell me how."

"At the moment, your ship is under guard. But the night after next, when everybody's celebrating, you would have a good chance of getting on board and slipping out of the harbour. I can arrange for the guards to get plenty to drink that night. You should find it quite easy to overcome them."

There was a moment of silence. Then the Norseman said slowly, "This is a good plan, but we cannot get from the castle to the ship. We will be seen."

"Oh, I can make sure everybody has other things to think about. You know that there will be fireworks that night?"

"I have heard this. What are these things called fireworks?"

"Big explosions, loud noises, huge stars in the sky. Everyone will be out on the parade ground in front of the castle, watching. And then I'll arrange for an even bigger explosion, and all the lights will go out. That's your chance – tell your people to be ready."

There was another pause. Harald said, "I will tell them. But not Valda. It is best if she does not know, not until we are going."

"You think she might refuse to go with you?"

"She is my daughter. She will obey me," he repeated, but this time he sounded less certain.

"You'd better make sure she does," Sir Kenneth said. "My only reason for helping you is to remove your daughter from Embra. If she tries to stay behind – well, I can't be responsible for her safety." There was an unmistakable threat in his voice.

"She will come with us. I will make sure of it. Thank you for your help, Sir Kenneth."

"My pleasure. And now Maxwell will see you back to your boat. I'll leave later on. It's best if we are not seen together."

I shrank down behind a barrow as the two men came out of the house. The man called Maxwell carried the lantern, but fortunately its light didn't reach me. Sir Kenneth must still be inside, in the darkened house.

I heard footsteps. He was coming closer. He stood just inside the window, almost within touching distance – I hardly dared to breathe.

What an evil man! He was meant to be helping King Andrew, but he was secretly working against him. He must have got used to having power, and now he didn't want to give it up.

I was glad I'd found out about this. I was also very scared. Of course I ought to try to tell the king, but it would be my word against Sir Kenneth's. Would anyone believe me?

18 Darkness

My legs ached from crouching down, but I didn't dare to move. I leaned my weight against the cold, damp wall of the house. The stones to build it must have been brought here from the aqueduct by order of Sir Kenneth. I wondered how much else he had helped himself to over the years.

Soon Maxwell came back with the lantern. I was hoping that Sir Kenneth would go down to the jetty at once. But he still had things to say to Maxwell.

"Our friend Harald thinks his daughter will soon forget King Andrew," he said. "I wish I could be equally sure Andrew will forget about her. But I don't believe he will. He's obsessed with the woman."

Maxwell said, "Do you think he'll try to get her back?"

"Yes. He believes that she loves him – the young fool! He'll think that her father took her away against her will."

"But, even if he sends out the entire navy, the Norsemen will have a good start. Most likely, they'll get away," said Maxwell.

"And if they don't? We can't have Harald telling the King that I helped him escape from Embra. That wouldn't do at all."

"No, sir."

"So I've thought of a plan. Tomorrow, when you go to inspect the Norse ship, take this book with you. Disguise it well – wrap it up and hide it in a food sack or someplace like that."

"*Weapons of War: A History,*" Maxwell read. "Is this a book from the king's library, sir?"

"It is indeed. We have copies, of course, but this is the original. It's one of the most valuable books we have, full of the secrets of the Ancestors. If it appears that the Norsemen stole it, the admiral will have every excuse to blast their ship out of the water. They will be called traitors and spies! People will ask, 'Is this how they repay King Andrew's friendship?'"

Maxwell laughed. "Very clever, sir, if I may say so. There's just one problem. Can any of the Norsemen read our language?"

"They wouldn't need to. The pictures in the book could show them how useful it would be. No doubt they plan to sell it to our enemies for a high price."

"Treachery! Vile treachery!" said Maxwell. "They deserve to die, sir!"

"Of course they do."

But Sir Kenneth was a traitor himself, twice over. He used people and then stabbed them in the back. He was a dangerous man to have as an enemy... even more dangerous as a friend.

Wouldn't it be safer to forget what I'd heard? Not even try to warn the king, but creep away and keep my mouth shut?

Sir Kenneth said, "It's time to go. Harald should be well clear of here by now."

The two men came out and headed for the shore. I didn't dare to move for ages. At last, when I was sure they must have left the island, I got up slowly. Stabs of pain went through my cramped legs.

The mist was even thicker now. I could hardly see the ground underfoot. I began to worry about getting lost between the islands, or even being unable to find my boat.

Stumbling through the darkness, I walked into a scaffold pole. This was no good – I had come back to the building again. I had gone round in a circle.

Then I stepped on something that creaked and broke underfoot. And I felt myself falling, falling...

I must have screamed. But there was nobody to hear.

I landed in water – cold, cold water. It broke my fall, probably saving my life. It wasn't deep enough to drown me. My feet could just touch the bottom.

In the blind darkness, I stretched out my hands and felt rocky walls all round me. I could only guess where I must be... down a well, a newly-made well. The workmen hadn't built a proper well head yet; they'd just covered the opening with planks. And I had fallen through.

Even though I knew it was useless, I shouted for help. Then I decided not to waste my energy. I would try to climb out and, if I couldn't, I would just have to wait until the workmen came back in the morning.

The sides of the well had been dug out of rock. I could feel rough places that might give hand and footholds, but the rock was damp and slippery. I managed to climb up a few feet. Then I lost my grip and slid back into the water.

It was cold – very cold. Maybe the water was too shallow to drown in, but the coldness could still kill you. I had to get myself above the water line.

I tried climbing the opposite wall. The handholds were better here. I went up quite a way, but then the rough rock changed to a smooth wall of bricks. It was no use – I couldn't climb any higher.

There was a narrow ledge, just wide enough to sit on, at the join of rock and bricks. At least I would stay out of the cold water, if I managed to keep myself awake.

The darkness was so thick that it seemed to press against my eyeballs. All I could hear was my own breathing and the slow dripping of water. I knew it would be a long time until daybreak.

And then, what if the workmen didn't arrive? It was the king's birthday. They'd probably been given the day off. They might not turn up the following day either, if they had had a lot to drink.

Or maybe – oh, no. Maybe work had stopped for the winter, as it had stopped on the aqueduct. Then I would never get out. I would starve to death.

I started to pray for help, but then I stopped. Why would God listen to me? I'd disobeyed the instructions in his book. I wouldn't even be on the island if I hadn't been chasing after Tom, thirsty for revenge.

It was all my own fault that I was here. I couldn't expect God to help me... if he even existed.

After a long, long time, a pale circle of light became visible high above. It seemed as far away as the moon.

I had been desperately hoping that, when daylight came, I might see something that would help me... a rope dangling down or some cracks in the brickwork. But there was nothing: only the steep walls above me, as smooth as the inside of a pipe, and below me the darkness.

All I could do was wait and listen hard, longing to hear the sound of voices. The small circle of sky turned blue; it was going to be a fine day for the king's birthday. Hours and hours went by, and nobody came.

I wondered what my friends were doing now. Ali would be on board the *Dolphin* – the king's ships were to fight a pretend battle offshore. Rob would be busy at the castle or in the High Street, where the king was providing food for a huge street party. Neither of them would have noticed I was missing.

Graham was probably enjoying a day off from writing. And Annie would have a rest too. For once, she wouldn't need to feed all the High Street beggars.

As I thought about Annie, some words she had read came into my head. "God knows everything about you. He even knows how many hairs are on your head! And he loves you."

Nobody knew or cared where I was, except God... if he was real... if he didn't hate me for going against his book...

But then, the book itself had said *"God is good to the ungrateful and the wicked"*.

I prayed out loud, my voice echoing in the depths of the well. "God, you're the only one who can hear me right now. Are you listening? I'm sorry I disobeyed you. If you get me out of here, I'll try to do better. I really will."

Then a strange thing happened. I'd been straining my ears to hear voices and now I heard one – not from outside the well, but quietly, inside my head.

"Don't be afraid, for I am with you."

With me? Even in the lonely darkness?

"I am with you. My strength will hold you up."

Now, surely, help would come! I listened eagerly. But all I heard was a sound like cannon firing far away.

As more hours went past and nothing happened, I thought maybe I'd been dreaming. Or else I had imagined the voice. That was more likely. Hunger and exhaustion could trick people into believing anything. Like the distant voice that seemed to be calling out my name – now that obviously wasn't real.

"Jamie! Jamie! Are you there?"

Wait, wait. Maybe it *was* real.

"Jamie! Where are you?"

"Here!" I yelled at the top of my voice. "Down the well!"

19 Fireworks

I couldn't have guessed who my rescuer would turn out to be. It was Tom.

He hoisted me out of the well, using some ropes and pulleys that the workmen had left. Never was I so glad to be in daylight, even though it hurt my eyes after so long in the dark.

Tom could see I wasn't fit to row back home. I hardly had the strength to walk down to the shore. He helped me into his own boat and hitched my one on behind it.

"You look like you need some food inside you," he said. "There's a pie under the seat that I never had time to eat – help yourself."

I ate hungrily. After a while, I felt a bit better, but I was still cold. Dampness and cold seemed to have got right into my bones.

"How on earth did you find me?" I asked him.

"You've got your boss to thank for that. Neil's been on the warpath, telling every boatman in Embra to look out for you. He said you stole his boat – took it out yesterday and never brought it back. So, when I came past here with a customer and saw the boat on the shore, I knew you must still be on that island." He hesitated for a moment... "Alive or dead."

"Why did you think I might be dead?"

"I thought... " His voice tailed off into an awkward silence.

"You thought Sir Kenneth might have seen me?"

"Yes. He's a dangerous man, Jamie. Don't tell anybody that you saw him meeting that Norseman. Just forget about it, right? I've had to forget a lot of things since I started working for Sir Kenneth."

His face was set as hard as stone.

I decided it would be safer not to tell Tom anything of what I'd heard last night. In fact, it would be safer not to tell anyone at all. I told him about exploring the island and falling down the well. He called me an idiot, but I was used to that.

"You saved my life, Tom," I said. "And look... I'm sorry I called you a thief."

Tom said, "Maybe you should ask Neil what happened to your money. Just a thought."

The stolen money was the least of my worries right now. In any case, when Tom dropped me off at the boathouse, Neil wasn't there. The whole pier was deserted. It was starting to get dark and Tom said everyone would have gone up to the castle to watch the firework display. He was going to pick up some passengers who wanted to see it from the water.

I walked up the High Street, wondering what I should do. Tell the king about Sir Kenneth's treachery? How exactly? Maybe, if I managed to find Rob, I could get him to write a letter and take it to the king. But he might not believe a word of it. And, if Sir Kenneth saw the letter...

I was so cold and tired, I couldn't think straight. All I wanted to do was to go back to my room, light the stove and get into bed.

The upper part of the High Street was crammed with people. They all seemed to be trying to reach the open space in front of the castle, which was already full. It would be impossible to reach the castle. I couldn't even get to the mouth of my close and, after a while, I gave up trying. At least I felt a bit warmer, squashed up in the middle of the crowd. Even if I collapsed with exhaustion, I wouldn't fall over.

The first of the things called fireworks went off with a sound like gunfire. It made me jump. A great fan of light, white and blue and gold, spread out over the sky, and the whole crowd gasped. Then came another one – different colours this time – and another.

How did those things get up so high, right amongst the stars? Graham might be able to explain it to me. They were probably an invention from the Old Times.

My granny always said it was unlucky even to talk about the Old Times. She wouldn't have been at all surprised by what happened next.

Suddenly, I heard people screaming up ahead – screams of terror, not excitement. Then I saw those white-hot lights, not up in the sky, but down at street level. And I smelt a horrific smell of scorching flesh.

One of the huge fireworks had landed in the crowd instead of going up into the sky. Down here it wasn't beautiful any more. It was deadly.

People panicked and ran. The street lights had gone out – nobody could see where they were going. I almost got knocked down and knew that, if I fell, hundreds of feet would trample over me.

Somehow I got myself to one side of the street and into the mouth of a close. I wasn't hurt, just dazed with shock.

Was this what Sir Kenneth had meant when he talked to Harald? Had he planned all this? A big explosion – the lights will go out – that's your chance...

I felt sick. Tom was right; Sir Kenneth was a dangerous man. He didn't care who got hurt, or even killed, as long as his plans were moving forward.

Maybe I could have stopped him. But not now. It was too late now.

When the crowd thinned out, I managed to find my way home. The long staircase seemed endless. At last, I reached my room, shut the door, and crawled into bed. I wanted to sleep. I wanted to forget.

"Jamie! Jamie!"

I woke from a confused, dark dream. Slowly, I realised that I wasn't down a well, but safe in my own bed. Somebody was banging on the door.

"Jamie! Are you there? It's me – Rob."

I got up slowly, with all my limbs aching and stiff. Something bad had happened yesterday... what was it? Oh yes, now I remembered.

I let Rob in. He wasn't in uniform and I realised it must be his day off. I ought to have met him at the café, as usual... but I had slept right through into the afternoon.

Rob said, "What's the matter – are you sick? I was worried when you didn't turn up. I thought maybe you'd got hurt last night when that firework went off. You know what people are saying? The Norsemen did it."

"No, it wasn't them. I know who—"

"It *was* the Norsemen. They got away in their ship. And they stole a book from the king's library! They were spies all along!"

"No, no. Listen."

I told him everything that had happened on the island. I had to say it twice before he took it in. Then he told me I must have been dreaming.

"Maybe this will prove it," I said. "I can tell you the name of the stolen book. *Weapons of War* – something like that. Sir Kenneth told Maxwell to hide it on the Norse ship."

He stared at me, open-mouthed. "You're right. It's got everything about guns in it and how to make gunpowder, and a lot of other stuff that our scientists are still working on. The king's librarian reported it missing this morning... just after the news came in that the Norsemen had gone."

"Sir Kenneth is very clever," I said.

"I can't believe he would do that!"

"I couldn't either. But I heard him say it with my own ears."

We talked about what we should do.

"You've got to tell King Andrew!" exclaimed Rob

"He won't believe me," I said. "Even you didn't believe me at first, Rob."

"All the same, we have to try." His face was grim. "We can't let Sir Kenneth get away with this."

20 Urgent message

Surprisingly, it wasn't hard to get into the castle. The guards at the outer gate looked as if they had a bad hangover from the night before. They waved Rob through the gateway, even though he wasn't in uniform.

"S'all right, son, I know your face," one of them said to him. "And this lad's a friend of yours? That's fine."

"They should have made me sign you in and say why you're here," Rob muttered. "That's what is supposed to happen."

We walked up the steep road that climbed the castle rock. A gusty wind was blowing. The flags along the battlements fluttered and flapped erratically. In the sky to the west, ominous clouds were piling up, as black as cannonballs.

"Looks like there's a storm coming," I said. "That's weird. It was a storm that brought the Norsemen here in the first place. Do you think their new mast will survive this one?"

"They've got more than the storm to worry about. The king sent out four warships to chase the Norse ship – the *Dolphin* was one. They sailed on the noonday tide. If they find that book on the Norse ship, they have orders to sink it with all on board."

"But what about the woman? Didn't you say the king was in love with her?"

"Yes, and he believed she loved him. Now he thinks she was pretending all the time."

"He's angry then?"

"Furious."

I remembered what Sir Kenneth had said about King Andrew. "The King is used to getting his own way... if people disobey him, he can be quite ruthless." Maybe it was true. Maybe the King was just as hard and selfish as Sir Kenneth. Was that what power did to people?

We had reached the inner courtyard of the castle. The guards here were more alert. They demanded to know our business.

"We have a message for His Majesty King Andrew of Lothian, to be delivered personally," Rob said in his most official voice. It was a pity he wasn't in uniform. Somehow the effect was not the same.

The soldier stared at us as if he didn't quite trust us. He called a servant, who recognised Rob, but frowned at me. I suddenly realised what I looked like - an Embra boatman in dirty clothes.

"You have a message for His Majesty?" the servant said.

"Yes," said Rob, "but it's highly confidential."

"He is in conference with Sir Kenneth. I will enquire if he will see you later. You'll have to wait."

We were searched for weapons – I was glad I didn't still have that knife on me. Then we had to stand in the courtyard for a long time. The sky was getting darker and darker, and I heard the rumble of thunder far away.

At last, the doors opened and Sir Kenneth came out, looking pleased with himself. He strode across the courtyard and entered another part of the building. "That's where he lives," Rob whispered. "He has a suite of rooms almost as grand as the King's."

"You should see the house he's building on that island," I said.

The servant appeared: "His Majesty will receive you now."

I was right – King Andrew didn't believe me.

"You must be mistaken," he said. "Sir Kenneth was my father's oldest friend. He's been my guide and helper ever since I came to the throne. He would not do this!"

"You shouldn't put so much trust in him, Your Majesty," I said. "Did you know he's building a grand house on an outlying island?"

"Of course I know about it," the king said angrily. "Is it a crime to build a house?"

"It is, if the workmen and the stones to build it were stolen from the aqueduct project," I said.

He looked startled. "Do you have any proof of that?" he asked.

"I took some of the stones there myself, in my boat."

The king frowned. He began to pace up and down the room. Outside, I could hear the sound of thunder much closer now.

"I cannot believe that Sir Kenneth would do all this," said King Andrew. "The badly-aimed firework – that was just a terrible accident. Two people were killed, and many were horribly burned. And you're telling me he caused it? No. It's impossible."

I said, "He knew about it the day before. He told Harald there would be a big explosion and all the lights would go out. That's exactly what happened."

"But how – how could he make such things happen?"

Rob said, "Sir Kenneth gives orders and people obey: either because they're afraid of him or because he pays them well."

"Or both," I said, thinking of Tom.

"Your Majesty, have you thought what this means?" said Rob. "If Jamie is right, the Norsemen were not spies. But, if our warships catch up with them and search their ship, that book will be found."

"Just like Sir Kenneth planned," I said. "Innocent people will be killed... again."

And one of them will be Valda. Neither of us said it – we didn't need to. On the king's face was a look of anguish and indecision. I could see that he half-wanted to believe me, for Valda's sake. But that would mean Sir

Kenneth, the man he'd trusted for years, was a cunning traitor.

He said, "I'll send for Sir Kenneth. I must hear what he has to say about all this. I'm sure he'll be able to explain everything."

My heart sank. "If you give him the chance to speak, he'll persuade you I've been telling lies. I just know he will. Don't listen to him!"

This was what I'd been afraid of. It would be my word against his – and the king would believe Sir Kenneth.

Suddenly, Rob said, "Do you have radio contact with the *Dolphin*, sir?"

"Yes."

"Well, can't you send new orders? Tell the admiral not to sink the Norse ship, but bring it back here. Then ask Harald Haraldson if it's true that Sir Kenneth helped him to get away."

The King's face brightened. "Good idea! That's exactly what I must do. I'll see to it at once."

Just then I heard a quiet sound... a door closing softly. The servant who had ushered us in had been standing by the door, unnoticed. Now he had left the room, without being told to. Was he on his way to tell Sir Kenneth what he'd heard?

"Come with me," King Andrew said to us. "I might need your help. I can't think straight." He looked worried. Normally, I guessed, Sir Kenneth would be at his side when decisions had to be made and now he was having to make do with two boys from the country.

We followed him up a spiral staircase to the radio control room, high up in the castle. The operator, who looked as if he had been quietly dozing, leaped awake and sat up straight.

"Any news?" the King demanded. "No? Good. We may still be in time. I have an urgent message for Admiral Crawford."

The window, which was open to let the aerial cable pass through, was suddenly lit by a flash of lightning. A few moments later came the thunder. The radio operator looked alarmed.

"Your Majesty, I have orders to disconnect the radio from the aerial cable if there's a storm overhead. The cable goes up to the highest point of the castle – the top of the flagpole on the tower. Lightning could strike it and run down the wire."

"What would that do?" asked Rob.

"Destroy the radio... and maybe kill us."

"We still have time," the King said. "The storm isn't overhead yet. Be quick, man! Are you ready to send?"

I was standing by the doorway. Instinctively, I felt I wanted to guard it, even though I had no weapons to use.

There was the sound of hurrying feet on the stairs. It was Sir Kenneth. He gave a swift glance through the half-open door and then hurried on upwards. What on earth was he doing?

The aerial. He was planning to destroy the aerial so that no message could be sent.

Without stopping to think, I ran after him. And the storm rumbled closer.

21 Lightning

The twisting staircase ran up the inside of the tower. I knew Sir Kenneth couldn't be far ahead of me. Then I heard a door slam shut.

The steps went up to the ceiling of the tower, ending in a trapdoor. That was the only door. Sir Kenneth must be outside, on the roof. But I couldn't lift the trapdoor. Maybe he was standing on top of it.

If he succeeded in destroying the aerial, the *Dolphin* would never receive the king's message. Harald would never be brought back to answer awkward questions about the past. And Sir Kenneth might manage to cling onto his position of power.

That is, if he didn't get killed first. The storm must be very close by now.

I banged my fist against the door. "Sir Kenneth! You're in danger! If lightning strikes the tower..."

There was no answer. He probably knew the danger he was in. How could a man be so desperate for wealth and power that he'd put his own life at risk?

Rob came running up the stairs. "What's going on?"

I told him what Sir Kenneth was up to.

"He's too late," Rob said. I could hardly hear him above a heavy drum roll of thunder. "The message got through – heard and understood."

I looked upwards. "Should we tell him? Or not bother?"

Rob shrugged his shoulders.

Then I noticed something: there was a bolt on the inside of the door. If I slid it across, Sir Kenneth would be trapped out there on the roof. With any luck, lightning would strike him. He'd be burned to death – just like the people hit by that firework.

I put my hand out, but then drew it back. I'd remembered something. *Do not murder.*

But he deserves it! Go on – do it!

For a long moment, I stood there, weighing things up. Sir Kenneth was a wicked man – surely God would want to punish him? If he was dead, there would be an end to his evil-doing.

Don't fight evil with evil. You can only overcome evil with good.

At first, I thought Rob had said those quiet words that sounded like something out of my book. But Rob was already on his way down the stairs.

I knew then what I had to do. I knocked again on the trapdoor and shouted as loudly as I could.

"Come down, Sir Kenneth. You're wasting your time – the message has got through. Come down!"

Then I ran down the steps. The last thing I wanted was to meet Sir Kenneth face to face.

In the radio room, Rob was already telling King Andrew what had happened. The king looked very angry. He strode to the window, leaned out and shouted to the soldiers in the courtyard.

"Guards! Up here – at the double!"

Then he stood on the stairs, grim-faced, waiting for Sir Kenneth to come down.

"Sir, I must ask you what you were doing up on the tower roof."

"Just checking that everything is in order, Your Majesty," Sir Kenneth said smoothly.

"On the roof, in a thunderstorm? Do you expect me to believe that?"

Sir Kenneth didn't answer. He was trying to edge past the King, to get down the stairs. King Andrew stopped him with an outstretched arm.

"Look out! He's got a knife!" Rob shouted.

The king leapt aside. The knife missed him by an inch. Sir Kenneth darted down the stairs – just in time to meet the guards running up.

"Seize him!" shouted the King. "Put him under arrest!"

"Get out of my way," Sir Kenneth commanded.

I could tell that the leading soldier was unsure what to do: obey Sir Kenneth or the King? Who was more important – more powerful?

He decided to obey the King. He drew his sword and forced Sir Kenneth back against the wall. Another guard grabbed the knife and between them they marched Sir Kenneth down the stairs.

"What will happen to him?" Rob asked King Andrew.

"He attacked me! I could have him executed right now!" The King's face was pale. "But I won't do that. He'll be imprisoned in the castle vaults. He must be put on trial for everything he's done."

Then he looked at me. "I'm sorry I found it hard to believe you. I know now that you were telling the truth – Sir Kenneth has just proved it himself."

Suddenly, Rob said, "What's that noise?"

A strange hissing, buzzing sound filled the air. At first, I thought it was coming from the radio – then I saw the machine had been disconnected and moved away from the window.

A weird, tingling feeling ran up and down my arms. My hair felt as if it was standing on end. Cold terror gripped me. What was happening?

The brightest light I'd ever seen lit up the window. The loudest noise in the world rocked the whole room. I felt as if my ears had burst.

But slowly, as the rolling of thunder died away, I realised that I was still in one piece. We all were.

"Did lightning actually strike the tower?" Rob asked, awestruck.

"Yes." The King didn't look at all worried. "It happens every few months. You get used to it."

"How come the tower hasn't been destroyed?" I asked.

The radio operator explained, "The Ancestors put in a metal rod to take the lightning safely down to earth. Lightning loves metal. We'll need a new aerial cable, Your Majesty, when the storm is over."

"What would have happened to Sir Kenneth," I said, "if he was touching the aerial when the lightning struck?"

"I'd say there would be very little left of him by now."

"Which might not have been a bad thing," Rob muttered.

Three days later, the admiral's fleet returned to harbour. The Norse ship was not with them. They'd failed in their mission to track it down.

"The storm did it," Ali explained to Rob and me. "We reefed all the sails, but we were still blown far out to sea. By the time we got back within sight of land, there was no sign of the Norsemen."

"Maybe their ship sank in the storm," said Rob.

"Or maybe they found shelter in an English port. We went as far south as Alnwick, but we didn't go into the harbour. The admiral said he wasn't going to risk starting a war with the English - not for the sake of a woman or a book."

Rob said, "But it's not just any old book. If the Norsemen find it and realise what's in it... "

We all thought about what this could mean. The book was from the Old Times. It described the weapons of the Ancestors; it was full of death and destruction. Now its secrets could be let loose in the world.

Ali said, "The next time we go to war, our enemies might have guns of their own."

"We'll just have to hope the book is drowned in the depths of the sea," said Rob.

"What about Harald and his people? They don't deserve to get drowned," I said, thinking of the Norseman who'd helped me.

Ali said, "Whatever happens to them, I hope they stay well away from Embra. That Valda woman caused a lot of trouble."

"I don't think the king will ever forget her," Rob said.

"That's what I mean," said Ali.

I went back to see Neil, my boss, to tell him I had a new job. I was to be one of the king's boatmen, part of the crew of the royal barge that carried the king around the city.

"I need trustworthy people around me," King Andrew had said to me. "Some of my staff probably served Sir Kenneth better than they served me. But you, Jamie – I know I can rely on you."

Although I was honoured to be given the job, secretly I wondered if I would like it. I was going to miss the freedom of rowing around the city on my own. And the uniform (blue velvet breeches and a three-cornered hat) was even worse than Rob's.

"Well, if you don't like the job, come back here," said Neil.

Suddenly, I remembered what Tom had said about my money.

"Er... I had some money put away in the boathouse. But it's gone now. You haven't seen it, have you?"

Neil looked surprised.

"Oh, so it was yours, was it? Why didn't you say?"

"Of course it's mine," I said angrily. "Who else would have put it there?"

"I thought it must be Donald's. He rowed that boat before you. He used to sleep in the boathouse too. He got knifed in a street fight – that would be why the money was still there, I thought."

"Well, where is it now?"

Neil took out a heavy sack of coins and counted out a small handful of them. "There you are – £50."

"But I had more than that. I had at least £100!"

"Aye, and half of it should have been mine! That was the agreement."

I wanted to hit him. Two things stopped me – one was the knowledge that he was right. I had agreed to give him half my earnings and I hadn't kept my promise. The other was the memory of those words from my book. *If someone takes your coat, let him have your shirt as well...*

Did that mean I should let Neil keep *all* the money? No, no! I quickly took the £50 and walked away.

I still didn't know who had robbed me that night in the close. Maybe I would never find out. Perhaps it had been a complete stranger, not someone I knew.

I had learned something – you could never really know people. Friends might let you down, good people could turn out bad, and enemies could sometimes be friends in disguise. But there was one person who would never let you down, as Annie had said. One who was always there, even in darkness and loneliness.

Graham had finished writing out my book. The book itself had gone back to the castle for safekeeping, but the copy – five written scrolls – was in the public library for anyone to look at. I sometimes got Graham to read bits of it aloud to me.

"It's a strange book," he said. "There are good things and bad things in it."

"Bad things?"

"I mean it's full of warnings. If people go on and on doing wrong, in the end, they'll be punished." His face was troubled.

"But the book says God doesn't want that to happen," I reminded him. "He wants everyone to be saved. If they listen to the warnings and come back to God, he'll rescue them."

In my mind, I had a sudden picture of Sir Kenneth up on the tower. Even Sir Kenneth, that evil man, had been given a warning and another chance. And even me, although I had killed someone...

"Anybody can come back to God," I said. "He loves us. He wants us to love him. It's all in the book."

"Yes. That book deserves to be better known. I'd write out another copy if I had the time. But they've given me a different book to work on now." He gave a deep sigh. "*Quantum Physics for Dummies*, it's called. I don't understand a single word of it."

I was told I would have to be a witness at the trial of Sir Kenneth. I had to ask what "witness" and "trial" meant – we didn't have such things at home on Insh More.

As the days drew nearer to the trial, I began to feel anxious. I wasn't looking forward to answering questions about the things I'd heard Sir Kenneth say. What if I couldn't remember exactly? What if I made myself look a fool in front of a crowd of important people?

But I needn't have worried. Two days before the trial, the news flashed around the castle like lightning.

"Have you heard? Sir Kenneth's escaped!"

Nobody knew how he'd got out of the prison vaults, or out of the castle itself. He must have had friends helping him, with plenty of money to bribe the guards. (Four of the soldiers on duty disappeared that same night.)

And nobody knew where he might have gone. He'd probably left the city. His face was too well known to be easily hidden there.

One thing I was sure of, though – he would be back. He loved power and influence. He wouldn't be content to live out his life in some country village. He would be back. And that would be bad news for King Andrew and for Embra.

As Ali put it: "Batten down the hatches. Get ready to reef the sails. There's a storm on the way."

Look out for the final book in the Lost Book Trilogy!

The Book of Life
Kathy Lee

A blind beggar brings a mysterious message to the King of Lothian. *An old friend needs your help...* This is the start of a dangerous mission, taking Rob and Jamie far from Embra to a land of darkness, slavery and death. Will they ever be able to escape? Can they still trust in God, even when he seems far away?

£4.99

978 184427 369 0

And have you read the first book in the *Lost Book Trilogy*?

What lies inside **The Book of Secrets**?
Kathy Lee
£4.99
978 184427 342 3

Want more action and adventure?
Try these great books!

A Captive in Rome

Kathy Lee

"Where's Father?"

Conan, my brother, looked up the hill, where our dead and dying soldiers lay like fallen leaves... hundreds of them, too many to count. Faintly in the distance I heard the sound of a Roman trumpet.

A disasterous battle tears Brin's world apart. Captured and taken into slavery, he is forced to start a new life in the incredible city of Rome!

£4.99, 978 184427 088 0

The Dangerous Road

Eleanor Watkins

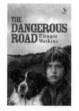

Gwilym and his dog Brown are on their first trip taking his father's sheep to market. They'd be having a good time if Huw, the old shepherd, didn't always want to spoil their fun. But soon the dangers of the drovers' roads threaten to put a stop to their fun, and their lives altogether.

£4.99, 978 184427 302 7

The Scarlet Cord

Hannah MacFarlane

Joshua is leading the Israelites towards the great city of Jericho. The army is getting ready to make its move. But on the plains in front of Jericho, four children are heading towards the greatest danger they have ever faced.

£4.99, 978 184427 370 6

Fire by Night

Hannah MacFarlane

Moses is leading the Israelites out of Egypt, but for two members of the tribe of Asher, things have gone badly wrong.

£4.99, 978 184427 323 2